Faith. Hope. Love

IHRILYN D. PENDATUN

WESTBOW
PRESS®
A DIVISION OF THOMAS NELSON
& ZONDERVAN

Scripture taken from the New King James Version®. Copyright © 1982 by Thomas Nelson. Used by permission. All rights reserved.

This is a work of fiction. All of the characters, names, incidents, organizations, and dialogue in this novel are either the products of the author's imagination or are used fictitiously.

WestBow Press books may be ordered through booksellers or by contacting:

WestBow Press
A Division of Thomas Nelson & Zondervan
1663 Liberty Drive
Bloomington, IN 47403
www.westbowpress.com
1 (866) 928-1240

Because of the dynamic nature of the Internet, any web addresses or links contained in this book may have changed since publication and may no longer be valid. The views expressed in this work are solely those of the author and do not necessarily reflect the views of the publisher, and the publisher hereby disclaims any responsibility for them.

Any people depicted in stock imagery provided by Getty Images are models, and such images are being used for illustrative purposes only. Certain stock imagery © Getty Images.

ISBN: 978-1-9736-2121-8 (sc)
ISBN: 978-1-9736-2120-1 (e)

Print information available on the last page.

WestBow Press rev. date: 2/26/2018

Contents

Dedication

To My Lord and Savior
Jesus Christ
To My One and Only
To everyone who believes
That true love never ends.

Prologue

Letting go

Letting go is so easy for some but not for me. I don't know but my heart is just so stubborn. I don't easily give up. It takes me a very long time to let go. My eyes can always see the other side of the story. A flicker of light in the candle gives me hope for a better future. But that was changed that Sunday afternoon when I communicated with him the feelings I've been holding on…the hurt that caused me so much pain that seemed to rip off my heart again and again. I've tried to hold his hands, but to my surprise, it felt cold. I knew that there was something missing. Well, perhaps the pain was so strong that my love was overshadowed by it. It saddened me to know that I felt that way. But I'd never been so true to my feelings before. I just don't know. I could justify everything that was out of standard but not that time.

Ending any relationship is really hard and devastating. I couldn't believe that I was thinking that way that time. Fear engulfed my heart. There were many "what ifs" in mind. And the thing was I didn't have the courage to say goodbye. It would be just fine if I'd be the one being left behind. I never saw myself saying goodbye. It was true that I've been so hard on myself. I'd been thinking of the feelings of others more than mine. My heart couldn't contain the feeling of hurting someone. In my mind, I knew that I should be kind to myself that time. I should give myself a chance to move on and grow…to be happy. For that one time, I wanted to decide for myself. I wanted to be true to my feelings.

I am Faith and this is my story…

CHAPTER 1

The Proposal

"So you're engaged!" Rachel exclaimed.

"Maybe. He just gave me this and yes, he expected me to wear this...the following day." I explained.

"You're supposed to be happy, right?" Rachel's eyes were searching mine as if looking for something. Rachel is my friend since college and if there's someone who really knew me, I must say that it's her. Aside from her "visionary" instinct, I can say that whenever I look into her eyes, she'll know if something is wrong.

"I don't know. I feel so confused. I am no longer sure, if pushing through this engagement is the right thing to do. I heard stories from a friend that things like these happened when they were planning their wedding. There was a time that she and her fiancé didn't talk for a month to clear things up. In the end they passed through the trial and now they're married for 6 years and have two kids." I shared to Rachel. I was explaining to her but I felt like I was the one who needed the explanation.

Deep in my heart, I don't know what would really happen. I'm not sure if we've been in the same situation. Perhaps they only got petty differences why they were able to patch things up and ended up together. I wished everything was as simple as that.

"You know what Rachel, I'm no longer excited for that day. I really thought that he was the one. But everything seems different and not right. Ever since we started to plan for the wedding, it seemed not right." I confessed.

"You must talk to him about this Faith. So it will not be unfair for both of you." Rachel said.

"Right, so it will not be unfair to him..." And to myself.

Time flew so fast. It's been three years. Maybe, some things are really meant to be and some are not. I decided to let go of that relationship. I didn't plan it though. And I really thought that we'd end up together, living happily ever after (like some fairy tales). But I guess fairy tales are not for me...or at least it was not yet time for me. Looking back, I realized that I didn't have the time to cry. Perhaps I was not able to feel the pain anymore. I was unsure. I got myself busy to study again. Rachel told me that she knew a school offering courses that I might be interested with. That must have been God's appointed time for me to pursue the path my heart really desired. By God's grace I finished the program offered and I was prepared to continue that path.

It was so different 15 years ago when the man I dearly loved broke up with me. I grieved for years. I just couldn't move on. I could still remember how I used to cry myself to sleep and woke up crying again. I wanted to be near his place so I could have the chance to see him. I even applied for works near his place so I'd be able to see even the gate of their village on my way home. I was really hoping to see him. But it never happened. Oh my! Why am I thinking about these things now? Of all places and time, why am I reflecting of the past while I am already rushing my way to Today's Hope.

"Faith!" I heard a familiar voice called me. I was walking and running in my rush to be at the center. I was really running late. I have a presentation to Ma'am Carmen regarding the children's book we are about to launch as part of the fund-raising to build a new home for boys of Today's Hope Center for Children. As I turned to see who called me, I saw Gabriel. I couldn't say a word. He looked different, though.

"Hey, get in, you don't want to be late right?" He said smiling.

"Why are you here? You said you're rushing the progress reports for the sponsors...? Have you finished? I curiously asked. He just smiled and signaled me to get inside the car.

"Everything was done last night. I already sent the reports to our sponsors. So I am here. I want to hear your book proposal..." He winked his eyes and patted my back. My hands suddenly got cold.

I knew Gabriel was an expert writer and the thought of him listening to my proposal stressed me out. I just wanted to help on the fund-raising and if we get this right, this would greatly help in building the new home for the boys of Today's Hope.

"Okay, thank you for coming," I said in my most formal voice. I was still unsure of him coming with me. Well, since Ma'am Carmen and the children knew him already because of the outreach we had here a year ago, I shouldn't worry.

As he was parking the car, I saw Ma'am Carmen and waved my hand at her. As Gabriel and I got out of the car, some of the kids came running to greet us. It was Saturday and all the kids were at the center.

Looks like they are more excited to see Gabriel than me.

CHAPTER 2

More Than Fairy Tales

As Gabriel and I passed through the pathway of the center, I couldn't help but notice the vacant lot beside the basketball court where the children play in the afternoon. I remember when Ma'am Carmen shared to me about their plans of constructing a new home for the boys in that area. It would not be a huge building but just spacious enough to accommodate the kids. The center wanted to have comfortable rooms for the children so they can move well.

There would also be a mini-study room, prayer room, and activity area. These children are for long-term placement in the center.

For months, my friends helped me in brainstorming, writing and revising the book proposal. They even found a publishing company where we can propose the book. And if they like the book, they would print it for free. They offered this upon knowing that this project was for raising additional fund for the children of Today's Hope.

In a moment, we'd know if the publishing company would accept this or not. Ma'am Carmen hugged me as I entered the receiving area, which also served as the living room of the children. The dining table and chairs were neatly arranged making the place ready for the meeting. Refreshments were being readied as well.

"We are so excited for this Faith. Thank you for the hard work." Ma'am Carmen said.

"Thank you also Ma'am Carmen for allowing us to help in our little way. We can do this... all for the children." I said with so much enthusiasm and hope.

"I'm happy to see you, too Gabriel. I'm really glad you came," Ma'am Carmen said as she tapped Gabriel's shoulder.

Gabriel helped Teacher Angelo in setting up the projector while I was bringing out the folders containing the proposal. After fifteen minutes, the representatives of AGM Publishing Company arrived.

"Welcome to Today's Hope!" Ma'am Carmen said as she shook hands with Ms. Mitch Rosario, the Marketing Officer and Mr. Joseph Reyes, the Head of the Publication Department.

"Please come in. Let me introduce to you Faith Perez, she's one of the volunteers here. She's also our presenter for this special project." Ma'am Carmen acquainted us.

"Finally, we met Faith. I heard so much about you. And I'm excited to do this partnership," Ms. Mitch said. She held out her hands. And as I reached for hers, I noticed that she threw a glimpse to Gabriel. She was a bit surprised but seemed pleased to see him.

"This is Gabriel. He's also one of our dedicated volunteers. He teaches the kids." Ma'am Carmen told Ms. Mitch.

Gabriel didn't tell me that he volunteered here. I suddenly realized the reason why the kids were so excited to see him.

In a while, we started the presentation. Teacher Angelo started with a prayer and Ma'am Carmen presented the humble beginning of Today's Hope. Then it was my turn to present our proposal. My hands were really cold. Before I stand, Gabriel gently squeezed my hands as if assuring me that everything will be just fine. However, it made me feel more nervous.

The working title of the book was "More Than Fairy Tales." It was about the dreams of the children foretold in fairy tales. It aimed to impart hope for a better future. Both young and old can relate to this because we believe that at some point of one's life, he or she believes in fairy tales. The children of Today's Hope will also contribute stories and artworks for this book. I didn't notice that I was about to finish the presentation. I was not sure if I delivered it well. They were listening attentively. The serious look on their faces wanted me to end the presentation quickly. I was right, the presence of Gabriel added more pressure on me.

"More than fairy tales in the book that we are presenting, the dreams of the children of Today's Hope will come into reality. This special project would inspire them to reach those dreams." My voice revealed my emotions as it slightly cracked as I closed the presentation.

"That was a good proposal Faith. Congratulations! Sir Joseph, do you have something to say?" Ms. Mitch commented and turned to Sir Joseph.

"Well, what can I say? Like what you just said congratulations. I like it very much. So when do we start this project?" Sir Joseph casually said.

I was not sure if I'd look at Ma'am Carmen or Gabriel. But they both stood up and we hugged each other.

Finally, we made it.

CHAPTER 3

Running After

Sunday afternoon. After church, I rushed my way to Esther's Home. It was a 15-minute drive from the church. I've been working here part-time. For eight years, I still feel so welcome, happy and fulfilled for the times I spent with the nice and good people working in this place. This has been also the best "coffee shop" I went into. And nope, they were not selling coffee. But the taste of coffee I have here is just so heart-warming. It's a 3-in-1 coffee but the taste is different when served and shared by the staff.

My life is slowing down here. And I really enjoy the coffee break. What made the coffee special? It's the people, I must say. This is indeed what I can call a special "coffee experience." I can feel the warmth, peace and love. Deep inside me, I knew that it's worth looking forward.

This is the journey that I've been taking for years now as I purposely live my life. Some just easily knew what they want to be while others just tag along in what life has to offer. As for me, I am probably one of many people living one day at a time. Honestly, I am not a planner. I am not good at using a planner (literally). A planner must be filled up before a certain event happens. But I am doing the opposite! It's true, as my friend Rachel always reminds me that I just let things happen. Well, in a way she is right. I only want to leave everything in God's hands, believing that He's really the one who knows which way should I go.

"Deep thinking again?" I was startled when Ate Dina suddenly spoke from behind. She was holding a tray with a cup of coffee, orange juice, box of cassava cake and plate. She carefully put down the tray on the table beside me. She gave me the cup of coffee as she sat on the chair just across the table.

I've known Ate Dina since I started working with Esther's Home. She's also been my friend and coffee buddy ever since. She's our home head and she's really excellent in managing the homes of Esther's Home. Esther's Home is a child-caring agency for orphaned, abandoned and foundling children.

"Well, not that deep Ate Dina. Thank you so much." I smiled as I pulled back my chair to face her. She sliced the cassava cake and put it on my saucer.

"We'd thought that you might not go down to join the outreach because of your paperwork, that's why I just brought you some cassava. There's more if you want. And you can bring some for your Mom, too." Ate Dina sweetly said as she started to drink her juice.

"This is good, it's not that sweet and I really like it." I stirred up the cup of coffee.

"So how's your book proposal yesterday?

"Everything went well Ate Dina. The publishing company accepted it and hopefully we can finish the book for a couple of months. We have draft stories from the kids and my other friends. Please continue to pray for this project." I excitedly shared to Ate Dina.

"That's really nice, I'm pretty sure that you'll be able to do it. Thank God!" exclaimed Ate Dina.

"God is really good. There are so many people who are so passionate and willing to share their talents to make this dream a reality." I said as I ate the last portion of the cassava cake.

"By the way, Faith, we'll be having our most awaited staff night this February, you're coming right?" She asked expectantly.

"Well, I think it would be great. I'm excited to see how others would dress up for this special night." I confirmed.

"So, you have a date on your mind?" She asked.

"Oh no, I'm afraid I'm coming on my own. Well, can I invite my best friend Rachel instead?"

"Doesn't Rachel have a date on that night?" Ate Dina asked.

"I will force her to come with me!" I said with much conviction.

We both laughed.

"All right, it's up to you who would you like to bring along, just be there. It's a Saturday and you have no work." She assuredly uttered. "Yes, I heard you right Ate Dina! Thank you." I almost shouted.

"Okay then, I'll leave you for a while. I have to prepare for dinner. You're staying for dinner, right?" Ate Dina said while putting the empty plate, glass and the cup of coffee on the tray.

"Oh, I'm so sorry, I'll have to meet a friend after my duty. But thank you for asking."

I was preparing the financial reports for the board meeting next week. After printing the reports, I placed them inside the folders making them ready for presentation. As I was closing my computer, I noticed my phone with several missed calls. I usually kept my phone on silent mode.

It was Rachel. I hurriedly called her to know where she was.

"I'll be at the Bag of Beans in 45 minutes Faith, I got stuck in traffic." Rachel explained.

"Don't worry, I'm still here at Esther's home Rachel. Be careful on your way. See you later." I told her. After finishing everything, I went downstairs to say goodbye to Ate Dina. As I went out from the office, the children were already playing outside. Almost all of them came running to hug me. They were always like that and who could resist them? I am not a hugger but these children deserved all the hugs in the world.

"Ate Faith, it's like this oh!" Gellie said while demonstrating to me how to hug. She was so cute and I couldn't help but laugh with her. She's already six years old.

"Gellie, Ate Faith has to go early this time. Let her go." Ate Leah, one of the housemothers reminded Gellie."

"Go ahead Faith." Ate Leah added.

"No worries Ate Leah, seems like I have to learn what Gellie has just taught me."

For the next minutes, I played with the kids. Gellie asked me to hug her a lot. The other kids invited me to walk with them from one end to another. We also have this mini "track and field" game. The kids would fall in line and after counting one to three; they'd run so fast and then return to where we started. I almost lose track of time and forget about my friend that I have to meet. I hurriedly bid goodbye to the kids and got inside my car just a few steps away from our play area.

Good thing my car was fixed. Yesterday I was not able to use it because of flat tire. I had to run literally for my appointment with Ma'am Carmen and the AGM Publishing. It was a blessing that Gabriel decided to drop by. I realized that I've been running after for many things for the past months to complete reports, proposals, and other activities. I'm just glad yesterday was an exception. At least for a while.

Running After

I can still face tomorrow
Expecting of great things to come,
Lord I'm giving up my heart's deepest desires
I'll be here listening for the steps I have to take.

Waiting for Your embrace
On my knees I will pray,
You are uncovering my eyes
To see beyond this day.

No longer will I run after
Of what's not meant to be,
Trusting as You carry me
To the place You want me to be.

I'll rest on facing tomorrow
Walking with You Lord,
Raising my empty hands
As You hold me Lord…
-Faith-

CHAPTER 4

One Perfect Day

It was past 6 pm. The coffee shop was not crowded and I easily found a perfect spot to park the car. As I was nearing the entrance door, Rachel waved her hand. She got our favorite spot. The overlooking view of the lake beside the window was just amazing.

"Faith Katherine Perez, finally you're here. I've been here for about an hour, you have to treat me!' Rachel kiddingly said.

I chuckled at her. I missed Rachel. I've been so busy lately. That's why we didn't hang out so often. We're just updating each other whenever we have time to talk on the phone at work.

"Rachel Anne Morales, I think you should be the one to treat me, I heard you're the new Business Manager of the school?" I teasingly said as I reached out my hand to congratulate her.

"Who told you that?" Rachel looked defeated.

"Let's just say I have my sources, my ever reliable sources." I intensely looked at her eyes.

"Okay, that's what I'm going to tell you, Faith, you just spill the beans!" She pretended to be hurt.

"Congratulations my friend!" I stated victoriously as I began to look at the menu.

"Let me see, I think I'll have tuna steak, rice and mango shake. And I also have blueberry cheesecake for dessert, Shepherd's pie and a cappuccino." I playfully said.

"Oh no, where's your appetite Faith! I'm so ashamed!" She rolled her eyes.

I just smiled.

"Alright, that's fine, just be sure to finish them all or else..." She threatened.

"Of course!" I assuredly said.

"I'll just have shepherd's pie and a green tea." Rachel said. She then placed our orders.

While waiting for our orders, Rachel and I began our endless chitchat from work happenings to family, Rachel's schooling (she finally decided to take her special education), church and even her new hobby, biking which I could never learn.

"About my new job as business manager, I'm not really confident if I can do it. I feel that I'm not ready yet for the big responsibility." Rachel shared with me.

"Why do you feel that way? The management gave you that responsibility because you are capable, skilled and most importantly you have the heart. And you're Rachel! Fight, fight, fight!"

"You're saying that because you're my friend!"

"No, it's not that. I'm your friend that's why I am confirming that they have chosen the perfect person for the job! Don't ever doubt yourself, Rachel. You're really good."

"That's why I really have to see you...Thank you, Faith."

"You're most welcome Rachel! I know you can do it."

We started to eat. Then suddenly a sweet music filled the coffee shop. A cute little boy shyly approached the table next to us carrying a single-stemmed white rose. He gave it to the young woman wearing a simple and casual floral dress sitting just across a young man. The little boy got so much resemblance to the man. If my guess was right, he was his little brother.

"Please say yes to my brother?" the little boy asked the young lady. The young lady held close the little boy while tears came running from her eyes. Then the young man rose up from his seat, pulled out a small crystal box inside his pocket and fell on his knees. Rachel and I were both speechless for this special moment happening right before us. If my calculation was right, I think both the young man and lady were on their late 20's.

"I've been waiting for this time to ask you. Would you mind spending the rest of our lives together?" The young man sweetly inquired. In silence, everyone waited for her answer.

"Yes, I don't mind spending the rest of our lives together," she replied.

The young man put the ring on the finger of the young lady in front of him. They tightly hugged each other. Everyone in the coffee shop applauded in unison and congratulated the couple.

"Hey Faith, are you crying?" Rachel sneered at me.

I hastily dried up the tears from my eyes with my hanky. Why am I crying? This is so not unusual of me. And sometimes it's embarrassing but I just can't help it.

"I'm sorry, I got carried away. That was so lovely, don't you think? What a way to end our Sunday evening. But Rachel, you're also crying!" I tried to say in a high spirit despite my monotonous voice.

Rachel and I finished our dinner. My cappuccino was served. Rachel got her green tea. We're about to go home and I excused myself to Rachel to go to the ladies' room. As I got up from my seat and find my way to the ladies' room, I saw one familiar face of a man sitting two tables behind our table.

It was Gabriel de Vega. His name really sounds like a brand of cologne to me. He was a schoolmate from the university and for almost three years ago we became officemates. I was about to pretend not to see him but he waved his hand at me. I waved back trying to put a smile on my face. He stood up.

"I am leaving, I'm with a friend," I explained.

"Yeah, I saw you a while ago." Gabriel said. He was here at the coffee shop that long. I hope that he didn't see me when the perfect proposal happened.

"So, how long have you been here?"

"I was here at around 5 pm. Remember the man who proposed? He was my cousin Lemuel. I'm here to support him."

"I see..." I just hope he didn't see my reactions while the proposal was happening.

"How's your car?" Gabriel inquired. He seemed so concern.

"Oh, good as new. Thanks to you. You saved me yesterday. I owe you one." After the book proposal, Gabriel helped me change the flat tire.

Three blocks away from Today's Hope Center for Children, the tire blew up. I decided just to run my way through the presentation and I was at that state when Gabriel came.

"By the way Faith, this is my friend Isabel. Isabel this is Faith."

"I'm happy to meet you Faith!" She held out her hand.

"Same here Isabel." I took her hand. I couldn't help but noticed how beautiful she was. I didn't know that Gabriel has a special someone. They perfectly looked good for each other.

"It's so nice to meet you, Isabel. Gabriel, I think I have to go. Well, actually, I think I have to run (pointing my way to the ladies' room). You both take care." I smiled and turn my back straight away.

"Okay, see you tomorrow Faith!" I heard Gabriel said from behind. I didn't bother to look back.

I rushed my way to the ladies' room. After some time, I went back.

I was glad Gabriel left already. I almost forgot about Rachel. Oh, my!

"What took you so long Faith?" Rachel inquired.

"I'm so sorry friend! Something came up. Okay, can we go now?"

"Yeah, would you mind me going to ladies' room this time?" I laughed as Rachel asked me. I'd suddenly become so insensitive. What kind of friend am I?

"Not at all, go ahead Rachel." I just waited silently watching the beautiful lake view outside the window.

It was a long day. The church was perfect. I'd finished my work and played with the kids. Rachel and I finally got our perfect dinner updates. I witnessed a perfect proposal. And I met Gabriel and Isabel. My heart was so full. I felt like it would break anytime.

CHAPTER 5

Catching Raindrops

I dropped off Rachel at her house. I really enjoyed the night. But my heart was still full. It was overwhelming though. Perhaps I was just surprised of what happened at the coffee shop.

After greeting my parents, I went straight to my room. This Sunday was so jam-packed. I just lied down on the sofa and as I closed my eyes, I could not help but remember what the worship leader in the church said about her rain experience. She said that God's love is like holding raindrops in your hands. One cannot just contain the raindrops in one's hand. It will overflow. That's how immeasurable and unending God's love is. We can only hold that much because it would never stop and end. I also believe in that. And I fell asleep contemplating those thoughts.

We held hands but I couldn't remember how it feels like. He said we could embrace though. It was so sudden that I couldn't remember how we looked like. I could only remember the touch of my face on his shoulders. The embrace was so gentle like a gentle breeze of the wind across the hall. As if time stopped and I could feel my chin on his shoulders. He then looking straight into my eyes and I had to look away. I thought I was just dreaming all along.

Monday morning. It was an activity in our company gathering.

Everyone formed a big circle and each one switched from one to another to give encouraging gestures.

I went straight to the Communication Room after the activity. I remembered that I have to check an email from Ma'am Shelly about an article for the website.

"We still have dessert and coffee!" I heard Pam from behind.

Pam had been my friend ever since I worked in the mission organization. We had the same way home, so we'd always went out of the office together. She would always wait for me even if I had to render overtime to finish editing. When she got married last year, although she still wanted to wait for me, I had to tell her that someone's waiting for her at home and I'd text her when I got home.

"I'll go back Pam, I just have to check on something," I answered back while running to the room.

I was point-blank staring in front of the computer for about five minutes. I opened my inbox and saw various emails. I clicked on the message of Ma'am Shelly containing the edited article for the website.

I read Ma'am Shelly's message:

> *Dear Faith,*
>
> *Here's the edited article entitled, "Educating Community Kids Through Supervised Neighborhood Play."*
>
> *I just added some points. The rest of the article is okay. Go ahead and upload it on our website. One more thing, I think I'll have to extend my leave, I'll be coming for next week. I'm so sorry. I'll assign you to cover the medical mission in Antipolo. I'll also email Gabriel so you two can cover it.*
>
> *Hope everything is well.*
>
> *Ma'am Shelly.*

I heaved a sigh. Of all people, why Gabriel? Perhaps I could ask Pam to replace me instead. I suddenly feel awkward after what happened a while ago with Gabriel. I was composing my reply to Ma'am Shelly when I heard someone opened the door.

"Here you go, you can have my part." Gabriel came with a piece of blueberry cheesecake on a plate and placed it on my table.

"You don't have to; I was about to go back." I protested.

"Everybody is looking for you, so I just bring it here. Would you like to have coffee?"

"Oh, I'll get it myself. This is too much."

"By the way Faith, have your read the email of Ma'am Shelly?"

"What email?" I pretended not to know.

"We're going to cover the Medical Mission in Antipolo this coming Saturday."

"Oh, that. I think I'm not available on that day, I should ask Pam instead." Pam just got in the Communication Room.

"Speaking of Pam, here she is. Pam, I have a big favor to ask." I pleadingly asked. I looked straight into her eyes.

"What is it Faith?" She was holding a cup of coffee and was about to give it to me.

"About the medical mission, can you come with Gabriel on Saturday. I have a previous appointment, a very important one. Can you cover for me?"

"Saturday, all right I think ...." Pam started to say something...

"Please... say yes Pam?" I cut her off.

"All right, I'll do it." She helplessly agreed.

I hugged her as if I won a jackpot prize. I could just saw Gabriel smiling at us. Pam whispered to me.

"What's going on Faith, are you sick or something?" She was surprised at me. I didn't hug so much.

"I'm not. I'm just glad you said yes. I really have to attend to something very important this Saturday."

"Okay Pam, so it's me and you on Saturday," Gabriel said.

I ate the dessert and drank the coffee. The day went so fast. We all concentrated on our respective works. I uploaded the article on the website and checked some write-ups from the program staff. Pam was also busy calling some suppliers and printing press for the coffee table that would be released for the organization's anniversary.

Gabriel was also busy writing and editing some materials. It was past 5 pm, Pam packed up. Gabriel also fixed his things and said that he had to go early. I was relieved though because we would not go home together.

"Faith, are you sure, you're not going yet. Looks like it would rain."

Pam told me. "I'm okay. I have to finish something. I'll be off in an hour. Please go ahead, Pam." I said.

Pam and Gabriel went out already. After an hour, I packed up my things. I checked first all the lights before going out from the Communication Room.

I took the elevator to go down. As I got off, I realized that I left my umbrella inside the drawer. I didn't want to go back so I just run my way thinking I'd be able to get a taxicab right away or be able to get a bus ride. The rain started to pour down. I had no choice but to find cover to the nearest waiting shed.

As I was waiting, I held out my hand to catch the raindrops. I wanted to feel each raindrops falling in my hands. I closed my eyes, fully aware that I was alone in the waiting shed to feel the sudden fall of the rain.

"Hey Faith, what are you doing? You're getting wet." I heard a familiar voice. I saw Gabriel holding his umbrella as I opened my eyes.

"Gabriel, what are you doing here?"

"I just bought some groceries, I saw you running a while ago. That's why I returned. Need a ride?"

The rain seemed to pour down really hard. I was hesitant but Gabriel took hold of my laptop bag and held my hand as we walked towards the nearby parking area.

"We need to hurry Faith," Gabriel said.

CHAPTER 6

Remembering The Past

The heavy rain poured down for the next couple of minutes. Gabriel said that we should wait for the rain to subside a bit. I had no choice but to agree with him. I was sitting silently in the passenger's seat as I tried to compose myself.

He handed me his white hanky to dry up the drops of water on my face. I'd been working with Gabriel for almost three years but I'd never felt so uncomfortable like this when he was around. I couldn't even look straight to his face. I was not sure if he felt the same way but it seemed that it was the other way around.

The rain began to stop and Gabriel started the engine of the car.

"We can go home now," Gabriel said.

"I think you can just drop me in the nearest bus stop so you can go home also." I immediately declined.

"Nope, I'll bring you home. Are you afraid or something?"

"Afraid of what?" Is he thinking that I'm afraid of him?

"Afraid that I might charge you taxi fare!"

We both laughed.

"So Faith, what's happening on Saturday?" He inquired.

"Oh, that, I'd go to Today's Hope on Saturday. Teacher Angelo called yesterday. He said the kids submitted their materials for the book. I'll check on them." I explained.

He just nodded. The traffic was not that heavy. In my calculation, we'd get home in an hour.

I was glad that he opened the music player. I concentrated on the bay side view that I was seeing outside the window of Gabriel's car. I was fascinated on how the leaves of the trees seemed to dance with the wind. I folded my arms as I slowly lay back my head.

"Hey, we're here." Gabriel's voice startled me.

I didn't know that I fell asleep while he was driving. That was so embarrassing.

"Oh, I'm so sorry...."

"No worries." He smiled sweetly. I didn't notice before that Gabriel had a lovely smile.

"Thank you so much for the ride. I owe you one."

I hurriedly came out from the car and waved goodbye.

"You're most welcome Faith. Good night." He waited for me to get inside the gate of our house.

I couldn't sleep. Maybe because I had a long nap inside Gabriel's car. It was one of my most embarrassing moments. I decided to open my laptop and check some emails. I opened my sent items folder. I went through it and noticed one email I've sent for so many years ago to an unknown email address.

And I read it.

"I've been feeling so low tonight. There are so many questions in my heart. Just almost four months ago, a very important relationship had to end. I had to let go but the pain was still in my heart. I'm still hoping for a reconciliation but circumstances showed otherwise. I feel so unloved, rejected and alone.

I just wanted to share my life with the love I found but eventually, it couldn't happen anymore. I still believe that God has a purpose and a perfect timing for everything. It's just that it's very difficult to move on.

Everyday was a constant struggle for me. I was holding back the tears in my eyes. I could only utter, "Lord, it's okay if I had to feel this struggle, this is only a season of my life, I will accept this for tomorrow I will face a different story...Please don't let me go...just don't leave me, Lord..."

I prayed that the God would take away the pain I have in my heart but still, it won't go away. I really don't know when will it end. I only believe that the Lord will let me understand and see beyond the situation...

Tonight my nephew asked me to watch a movie with him. My heart really ached but I couldn't ignore him. It was almost 9 pm. My eyes just reminded me to sleep. But whenever I'd close my eyes; my nephew would threaten me not to sleep reminding me how beautiful the movie was.

Then I'd watch the movie again. Then, came the part that the good person and the villain had this conversation. The villain happened to be the roommate of the famous inventor, Louise and he said that he was the little boy, who never sleeps because of Louise's invention works every night. Louise would always stay late at night.

One night, Louise finished his invention, for the science fair. On the other hand, Moorhead would have his baseball game the next day. What happened was Moorhead, due to lack of sleep, slept literally at the game and their team lose the game. Moorhead's teammates had beaten him up. He never forgot what happened.

He blamed Louise from that day on and no one adopted him until he grew up because during the interviews he would always show his bitterness over what happened. He blamed Louise and promised himself that he would ruin Louise life. Until one day, Louise made two-time machines. Moorhead stole one of the time machines and went back to the time of science fair where he planned to steal Louise's invention. He indeed went back to the time when Louise was in the science fair and stole Louise's invention. He blamed Louise for everything. He didn't move forward like what Louise did.

"It's not my fault, it's just that you have to keep moving forward," Louise said to Moorhead.

Keep moving forward. How I wish that I could simply move forward at this moment. Right now...just like in the movie.

I am not sure if I can move on easily. I'm not sure if moving forward is easy. Perhaps I just need to still believe and wait for a happy ending. At least now, I am awake in the fairy tale I dearly placed in my heart. Yes, I didn't end with my first love. I was blaming myself. Maybe I must learn to forgive myself first so I can move on. One day I will hope again, love again and wait for a happy ending.

I didn't notice my tears were already falling from my eyes as I finished reading the email. It was written 15 years ago. I smiled at myself. I have to thank my nephew for asking me to watch Meet the Robinsons."

Sometimes, God would really speak to us in unique ways. The Lord spoke to me through my nephew that night. I decided to forgive and forget all the bitterness of the past. I started to keep moving forward. Until now.

Why am I becoming so emotional, remembering the past? Oh my, perhaps because of the rain. I hope tomorrow it would not rain anymore.

I dried up the tears in my eyes.

CHAPTER 7

Missing The Perfect Fit

It was already 8:25 am. I hurriedly opened the door of the Communication Room. We have a meeting with the HR Team in 10 minutes.

No heavy traffic today. But on my way to the office my favorite brown sandals tore down. I had no choice but to get a replacement. In my hurry, I bought a pair of shoes in a shoe store on my way. My right foot fitted perfectly and I asked the sales lady to wrap them immediately without realizing both were for the right foot. When I got to the office, I was dismayed to find out my carelessness. I could only blame myself for not taking the time to check on the shoes. Good thing, Pam had a spare of slippers kept in her drawer.

"Pam, I need your help..." I came to her right away.

"Oh good morning, Faith. What's the commotion?" She joked.

"I bought a pair of shoes and I got the wrong pair. I handed them to her." I seriously said ignoring her comment.

"What, this is so ridiculous." Pam started to laugh.

"Yes, I know. My sandals got tired of me and I had no choice but to let it go." This time I pretended to be so hurt.

"All right, you can use first my slippers." She pointed to her drawer.

I hastily got the slippers. I grabbed my notebook and pen, then I went straight to the Conference Room. The HR team, Ma'am Anne, the HR Manager, Ms. Marie, the Admin Officer and Lane, the HR Officer were already there preparing for the meeting. Ate Valerie, the Admin. Assistant had just arrived. Ma'am Shelly was supposed to be in this meeting but she was still on leave.

"Where's Gabriel, isn't he coming?" Ma'am Anne asked me.

"Oh, Gabriel is not here?" I asked back.

Gabriel never came to work late. He was one of the early comers in the office. I was about to go back to the Communication Room to ask Pam. However, as I opened the door, Gabriel stood right before me.

"Good morning everyone! I'm so sorry I am late…" Gabriel greeted.

I just returned back to my seat and Gabriel sat beside me. I slowly moved away to make sure I had enough distance away from Gabriel.

Lane opened the meeting with a prayer. Ma'am Anne reviewed the minutes of the previous meeting.

"Alright guys, so for our organization's retreat, that's scheduled on September 28th up to 30th, our final venue would be in Antipolo. Ate Valerie already contacted the account manager and she'll take care of our food for the three-day retreat. This is going to be good for sure. For the program, it would be Lane, Ma'am Shelly and I. For the logistics, transportation and room assignments, Marie, Faith and Gabriel are assigned. So any update? Who's going to start?" Ma'am Anne excitedly asked the team.

"Ma'am Anne, I'll go first." Ate Valerie raised her hand.

"All right, please go ahead…"

"Thank you. The menu is finalized already. And there will be a food tasting this coming Saturday, so somebody must go. The account manager will email the contract today." Ate Valerie said.

"Marie, can you come with Ate Valerie on Saturday? I'll ask Kuya Dello to drive you both." Ma'am Anne looked at Marie.

"I can do that, but I think Kuya Dello has a follow-up medical check-up on Saturday," Marie answered.

"Oh, I see. We'll get back to you." Ma'am Anne said.

Gabriel raised his hand.

"Ma'am Anne, I'll have a schedule on Saturday in Antipolo, I can probably drop off Marie and Ate Valerie at the venue?" he suggested.

"Sure, we're settled then. Thank you for your kindness Gabriel." Ma'am Anne replied.

"That's fine, it's along the way," Gabriel said.

"How about the program Lane?" Ma'am Anne asked.

"I've already drafted the program. I'll email you and Ma'am Shelly," Lane answered.

"Ok, that's fine. How about your group Faith?" Ma'am Anne inquired.

"I think, we have the complete list of the materials needed and if you still have additional supplies that we need to buy, please let us know," I said.

"For the room assignments, I still need to finalize it," Marie added.

"How about the transportation?" Ma'am Anne asked.

"We're thinking to rent two buses so everyone would be comfortable," Gabriel said.

"All right, that would be good. Just let us know the costs so we can finalize the budget for Finance," Ma'am Anne concluded.

The meeting lasted for two hours. After the meeting, I quickly returned to the Communication Room and concentrated on my work. I was really bothered by the unpaired shoes I bought that morning. I needed to return to the shoe stall after office or by tomorrow morning.

"Faith, Faith, it's lunch time...you're in deep thoughts again or you're thinking about your shoes?" Pam said. I didn't hear her at first. I gestured that she'd lower her voice a bit. I saw Gabriel raised his head.

I was about to stand when Gabriel approached us. He put a box of chocolate roll on my table. Pam and I looked at each other.

"That's very sweet Gabriel, how about me?" Pam teasingly said.

"It's for both of you. But it's not for free though!" Gabriel exclaimed.

"Oh no, I thought it's for free..." Pam looked disappointed.

"It's free if I'll get a cup of black coffee." Gabriel demanded.

"That's so easy Gabriel! Faith you can do it. You're the expert." Pam looked at me, expecting me to do it right away.

"Well, one black coffee coming..." I finally stood up. I just wanted to end the conversation.

"Chocolate roll and a cup of black coffee, seem perfectly made for each other," Pam said in her most poetic tone. Here she goes again. The writer within her was coming out again. Why do writers have so many interpretations on things?

I went to the pantry room to get the coffee. I got three cups for us. I didn't notice that Pam and Gabriel followed me. They already got some food for lunch.

"Faith, we don't have to go out to buy food. Look, Gabriel brought us." Pam said as she started to arrange the food.

"It was my mother's birthday yesterday that's why I have the cake. Then just this morning, a friend brought this chicken curry. We cannot consume this all at home so I brought them." Gabriel said.

I suddenly felt guilty. Yesterday was his mom's birthday. I understood why he got off early but why did he still insisted to drive me home? I was sure he got home late yesterday. I knew that I need to say sorry.

"I am so sorry Gabriel about yesterday, I didn't know that..." Gabriel cut me off.

"That's okay, come on let's eat."

"Who brought you this chicken curry so early in the morning?" Pam casually asked him.

"My friend Isabel..." he answered back.

Isabel. I remembered her. She was with Gabriel at his cousin's proposal. After eating our tasty lunch, Pam and I washed the dishes. Of course, we exempted Gabriel to do the dishes, though he insisted.

"Pam, let's go out together after office. I need to go back to the stall to change the shoes." I said.

"Sure! Would you like me to go with you?"

"Wow, that would be nice! Thank you."

"I'll help you find your perfect fit! Actually, your perfect fit is right there waiting in the Communication Room." Pam meaningfully said to me.

"What?" I asked.

"I mean the other pair of the shoes that fit you, it's right there in our room.'

"That's right!" I said.

"Ok, I'll make sure you'll not miss again your perfect fit later."

We went back to our room.

CHAPTER 8

Holding The Pieces Of Our Hearts

P am accompanied me at the shoe stall. The sales lady apologized for what happened. She even offered me to choose another style that I might like. I tried to choose another style, but I ended up with the same shoes I bought earlier.

"This is so you Faith. Choose another color. Let me see, purple or yellow? Try this." Pam tried to convince me.

I must agree with her. I would always choose black, brown, or white.

"I'm okay with this Pam. This is my perfect fit. Finally, they're together once again." I winked at her.

"Faith, are you referring to the shoes?" Pam seemed like driving at something else.

"Of course, it's about the shoes, is there anything else?" I answered back.

"You seem to like talking about something else!" She rolled her eyes and I pinched her nose.

Pam was playful at times and I really love her. We can talk about everything under the sun and most of the times we'd lose track of time just by talking.

"Pam, someone's waiting for you at home, unless you want to come with me?" I reminded her.

"Oh, that's right. I almost forgot!" She just raised her hands.

I waited for her to get a bus ride home. When Pam got married last year with Ryan, we got opposite ways going home. I decided to ride in a van on my way home.

Pam used to ask me why I was not bringing my car to work. She said it would be more convenient doing so. I explained to her that I was more comfortable riding a bus or a van because I could continue my sleep while on a ride unlike driving my own.

"Just give me a message when you got home Faith." Pam waved good bye.

"I will don't worry. Take care, Pam. Regards to Ryan!"

"All right, see you tomorrow Faith!"

Pieces of Our Hearts

I couldn't forget the look in your eyes
Whenever you stare at me at times.
I couldn't forget the touch of your hand
Whenever we had to bid our goodbyes

I wonder if you're all right,'
Are you feeling alone?
Is there someone taking care of you
Or making you laugh like the way I do?

Are you still singing the song we dearly love?
Whenever you couldn't sleep at night
Will I ever wipe your tears away?
Or just hold your hand when you are afraid?

Will I ever see the smile on your lips?
Your eyes as if saying you will never leave
Will the dreams we made still come true?
Or be also forgotten like the way you do

Will we find our hearts back home again?
Fulfilling the life we once dreamt of
As time heals the wounds that break our souls
Will love find us still believing?

Perhaps one day God will allow us
To meet again and make things right
So I will pray now for the strength to let go
For Him to take good care of you

To seek His will until that day comes
When we had found the
missing pieces of our hearts.
-Faith-

I smiled after reading the poem. After so many years, it was only this night that I tried to open the small box of shoes I kept in my drawer. I remembered putting inside this box every memory I had from my past. Some were good memories and some were not. I promised myself not to open this box until the day I am ready.

I was reading the stories submitted for the "More Than Fairy Tales" book for Today's Hope when I remembered to put the shoes I bought at the lowest drawer of my cabinet. I saw the shoe box I kept many years ago. I thought that maybe it was about time for me to open it again. I saw my small green notebook. I remember writing poems in here filled with thoughts, feelings, pains and struggles. I also saw some journal entries that I cut out from my journal book, simply because I didn't want to remember the things I wrote there.

I read an entry.

I saw Daniel today after my four years of waiting. I got out from the van when I heard him called my name. I didn't know what to say. He asked me where I was going and I just said that I was on my way to the office just across the street. He was also working in the nearby building. I hurriedly run to the office. I've been waiting for this moment to see him.

Daniel called at our office. I didn't know where he got my number but I could hear my heartbeat so fast. He asked me if I am already with someone else.

I wanted to tell him that I was waiting for him. But I didn't have the courage to say it. I've learned that he was in another relationship. But he confessed that his love for her was fading away. He described her as someone who had so much similarity in me.

He asked me what he should do. If it would be better for him to break up with her. It was hard to answer because I still love him, he was my first love and I dreamt of spending the rest of my life with him like what we had promised before. I wanted to tell him that I am still here.

But I didn't do that. I told him to remember the first day he loved her every time he would feel that his love for her fades away. He asked me if we could see each other but I opted not. My heart seemed to shatter into tiny pieces again. I wanted to see him but I was not sure if my heart was ready. And I didn't want to hurt anyone. I knew that feeling.

I knew that it was the right thing to do. Maybe we're not really meant to be. He was not my fairy tale.

That scene flashback in my mind. But as I looked back, if given another chance, I would still do the same. I may not end up with my first love but I had found an everlasting love in God. During those times, I came to know God more and more. And the more I seek to know God, my heart started to change. I understood the true meaning of love. Love is a sacrifice. Love is not about me, him or us. It's really about God. I knew I found an unfailing Love. And this love never ends.

The missing piece of my heart was not with Daniel. It was with God all along. He was holding the missing piece. And I didn't have to wait anymore.

I was not able to hold back the tears from eyes. But this time, I knew that these tears were for my God, my unending Love.

I returned the box to my drawer. I was indeed ready to open that box of my past memories. I had moved on. God is so good!

CHAPTER 9

The Serenade

"How many should we buy?" Rachel was referring to the Cornetto ice cream when she asked Aimee.

"Twenty-five pieces Rachel." Aimee replied. I overheard Rachel and Aimee talking while I was looking for the juice drinks. Before we went to the convenience store, we ordered food in the nearby food chain.

My phone rang. It was Justin.

"Hey Justin, where are you? We're all here at the convenience store," I told him.

Rachel and Aimee were already waiting for me at the counter to pay for the Cornetto. I hurriedly came to them to give the juice drinks.

"I'm almost there, Faith." I saw him approaching the door of the store.

"You're just in time, I'm so proud of you!" Aimee teased Justin.

They were really close since college. Justin got the paper bags filled with Cornetto ice cream and juice drinks from Rachel and Aimee.

"Let's go ladies!" Justin said as he led the way out.

We arrived at Today's Hope Center for Children at 8 am. We went early to spend time with the kids before checking on the stories and artworks they submitted. I also brought with me some stories contributed by other friends for the book. Pam and Gabriel also emailed stories for this book project.

"Good morning Teacher Angelo!" We all greeted Teacher Angelo when we went inside the center.

"Good morning everyone, I'm so happy to see you all." Teacher Angelo said.

"Good morning Ate Faith, Ate Rachel, Ate Aimee and Kuya Justin!" The children welcomed us. They just finished eating breakfast.

The children gathered at the receiving area after washing the dishes.

"Kuya Justin, would you like to hear our rap composition?" Wesley asked Justin. Wesley was 16 years old. He once lived in the streets until Today's' Hope rescued him. He's in second year high school now.

"Wow, I like to hear that!" Justin agreed.

"We'd love to hear it too," Rachel said with much excitement.

The children arranged the chairs facing us all. They sat one by one and Wesley led the rap. Ron, 13 years old was on the beatbox, and Zaldy was the second voice.

"One, two, and three..." Wesley started.

(Wesley)
"Today, the Lord has proven again
He is our only strength in everything.
Praise Him, for His goodness and mercy.
He restored our souls and spirits.

(Zaldy)
We were rejected by people around us
Even the people we cared and loved
But God saved and accepted us
He gave us hope and another chance

(Wesley and Zaldy)
God gave us unending love
That dwells within us now
We're here to share this
To everyone whatever it takes.

(Wesley)

People would see
Our new lives now
We will follow the path
The Lord set before us

(Wesley and Zaldy)
We praise God
He never gave us up
He knows us by name
He holds our hearts.
Forever we will praise our God."

That was so beautiful. These children were just so amazing. I was holding the tears from my eyes. But when I turned my back, I saw Justin drying up his eyes.

"Good job!" Justin commended the children.

"Thank you Kuya Justin!" the children replied.

"More, more..." We all urged the children.

"Kuya Justin, you should join us." Wesley suggested.

"All right I think I can do that! But what's the title of your rap composition?" Justin inquired.

"We titled it "Serenade," Wesley said.

They were singing and laughing with each other. They sometimes urged me to sing but I really couldn't sing. Well, I happily joined them in the laughing part.

After some time, we had to end our activity to start checking the materials for the book project. Justin and Rachel concentrated on the artworks while Aimee and I read the stories. We had 18 stories. Aimee and I agreed to write two additional stories.

"Faith, the food is here already." Justin called.

The food delivery was on time for lunch. We ate together with the kids. They really enjoyed the food especially the Cornetto ice cream. Teacher Angelo also prepared cassava cake and coconut juice.

The rest of the afternoon became busy for the four of us. At around 5 pm, we packed up and said good bye to the kids and Teacher Angelo.

Ma'am Carmen was not at the center. She visited the Open Day Center of Today's Hope in another town.

"Teacher Angelo, I will just update Ma'am Carmen about the progress of our work here. I'll try to email her tonight," I said.

"Okay Faith, that's fine. Thank you so much for your hard work. This means a lot for us," Teacher Angelo said.

"Oh no, the joy is ours. We'll go ahead now, and we'll see you again," I said.

"Wait Faith, you should bring the cassava cake!" Teacher Angelo said while giving to the four of us the packed cassava cake.

"Thank you so much!" Justin said.

"Thank you!" Rachel and Aimee said in unison.

We decided to go the coffee shop after we completed our work in Today's Hope.

"I missed this place!" Justin exclaimed as we walked in the coffee shop. The overview of the lake was just so amazing.

Aimee and I went to the ladies' room first while Rachel and Justin find a table for all of us. When we returned, I heard beautiful voices singing with guitar accompaniment.

"Oh no, don't tell me another proposal is about to happen!" I whispered to Aimee.

"What? Wait a minute. Is it...?" Aimee was so surprised.

"Rachel and Justin?" We said almost in unison.

We almost ran to approach the table. The group was singing the song "It might be you."

The song ended. Aimee and I were confused and excited at the same time.

"Do you have any song request?" The singer inquired.

"That's enough, for me, unless they want to have another song?" Justin pointed to us.

"I am okay with it!" I nodded.

"Another song please?" Aimee requested.

Aimee requested her favorite song "Realize" by Colbie Caillat.

The chorus says, "If you just realize what I just realized. Then we'd be perfect for each other, And we'll never find another. Just realize what I just realized. We'd never have to wonder if we missed out on each other..."

"Lovely song! Thank you." Aimee said to the band.

Then it was time for us to confront Justin and Rachel.

"So, are you two? When did this happen?" I crossed my arms when I asked them.

Rachel and Justin just laughed.

"Oh no." They both denied.

"The band started to sing here every Saturday. So they'll serenade customers like us." Justin explained.

"I see, I thought I miss out something here," I said.

"Same here," Aimee agreed to me. And we had high five.

"That's not possible ladies!" Rachel concluded.

"Yes, once a friend, always a friend!" Justin seconded.

We placed our orders. We just laughed and updated each other. As I watched how Justin cracked a joke and how Rachel would laugh, I couldn't help but think that if there'd be one person that I'd bet for Rachel, it would be Justin. Justin could have been perfect for her. I was hoping that they'd realized it someday. They could be perfect for each like the lyrics of the song that Aimee requested a while ago. I felt like I was having a last song syndrome here. Enough already. I laughed at myself.

But of course, I will not play like a matchmaker to them. I knew that Rachel has been praying for her God's will. If only I could tell her that the man he's waiting for was already in front of her. But I would not do that. I still believe that love will find a way.

I could sense Justin was not yet ready for a relationship. That was why I think Rachel and Justin would be a perfect couple in God's perfect time. Rachel described him as an ideal man. He's responsible, kind, good-looking, meticulous, family-oriented and most of all he has unwavering faith in God.

I was just observing them. Aimee. Rachel. Justin. How blessed I was to have them as my friends. Aimee was already married while Justin, Rachel and I chose to be singles still. They'd been my friends since college. Though we had our different endeavors, we'd still find time to meet especially if we have special projects.

It was really true, not all angels have wings. And I didn't have to look for them. They were right here with me.

I ate the last bite of the chocolate cake and started to drink the black coffee I ordered. Rachel was surprised because I didn't order blueberry cheesecake and cappuccino.

I just missed the taste of the chocolate roll and black coffee I had with Pam and Gabriel last time.

CHAPTER 10

Finding The One

"Here you go." Gabriel put a box of raisin cookies on my table. "Oh, what's this for?" I asked. I wanted to tell him that he was starting to have a habit of bringing food."

I got it from Antipolo," he casually said. "I thought somebody gave it to you again," I told him. He laughed.

"It's okay to say thank you," Gabriel said.

"That's right! And a cup of coffee would be great!" Pam said. I didn't notice her coming inside the Communication Room. Gabriel nodded. He also handed Pam her raisin cookies.

"All right!" I said sounding like defeated. When I came back, Ma'am Shelly was already in the office.

"Good morning Faith!" She greeted.

"Good morning Ma'am Shelly!" I said while putting down the tray of coffee.

"Since everyone is here, let's have a short meeting then?" Ma'am Shelly requested. Gabriel, Pam and Ma'am Shelly proceeded to the wooden center table. I went back to my table to get my notebook and pen.

"Okay, let's start the meeting," Ma'am Shelly gestured me to sit on the vacant seat beside Gabriel.

"So, how's the medical mission last Saturday?" She asked Gabriel.

"Everything went well Ma'am Shelly, we only missed Faith," he said. I felt my face turned red as Gabriel said that.

"I agree, Faith we missed you there!" Pam said.

"I'm so sorry, I really got an appointment that time. Well, I think I'll make it up to you for the next activity." I apologized.

"Okay, just do the write-up for this activity, Gabriel. How about our organization's retreat? Any update?" Ma'am Shelly continued.

"We had a meeting last time with the retreat committee. Guess, we're all set for it," I said.

"I'll assign the three of you for the documentation of the retreat. If that would be all right?" Ma'am Shelly asked.

"Sure, no problem!" We agreed.

"By the way Ma'am Shelly, I'll be out today. I'll cover the Youth Session in our Laguna Center," Gabriel reminded Ma'am Shelly.

"Oh, that's right. So who's coming with you?" Ma'am Shelly asked.

"I'm with Ate Liza," Gabriel said. Ate Liza was the Program Officer assigned to Laguna area.

"Any of you ladies coming?" Ma'am Shelly inquired.

"I am afraid I can't come this time. I have to check on the coffee table book." Pam replied.

I was about to say something when Pam cut me in.

"Faith can come, right Faith? This is the best time for you to make up for not coming at the medical mission?"

"Huh? I have to do some proofreading and editing..." I said.

"I think Pam is right, let me have that Faith. I'll do the proofreading and editing. You can come with Gabriel. He'd be needing help in the coverage." Ma'am Shelly reiterated.

I had no choice but to follow Ma'am Shelly. Ate Liza went to our office and informed us that we'd be leaving in fifteen minutes. I shut down my computer and get my backpack. Gabriel, on the other hand, got the camera from the storage room. As we were approaching the elevator, Ate Valerie called.

"Faith, phone call!'

"Who is it?" I asked.

"It's Justin, your friend!' Ate Valerie said.

"I'll follow you at the car park Gabriel," I told Gabriel.

"All right," Gabriel said.

I hurriedly came down to the car park after talking with Justin. But to my surprise, Gabriel was still standing near the elevator.

"I thought you go ahead?"

"It's all right, I'm waiting for you. Ate Liza went to the ladies' room."

"Thank you, Gabriel."

"I'm glad you're coming with us Faith," Ate Liza said.

"Yes, Ate Liza. I'm coming with you!"

Gabriel got my backpack and placed it on the back seat. He opened the passenger seat and gestured me to get inside the car. I was planning to sit on the back so I could sleep during the two-hour travel but I guess my plan didn't work out.

I slept late the night before to write a story for "More Than Fairy Tales" book. But still, I just couldn't write anything. Probably, coming to the activity might give me something to write. I was hoping though.

On our way, Ate Liza gave us sandwiches and drinks. She was always like that. Suddenly Gabriel's phone rang. It was Isabel.

"Hello Isabel, I'm good. I am driving my way to Laguna. Can I just call you back?" Gabriel said.

"All right, thank you. I'll call you," Gabriel said as he ended the call.

He concentrated on his driving. I asked Gabriel if I could just open the window beside me so we could breathe some fresh air.

"Can I open the window?" I asked him.

"Sure," he said. I was becoming uncomfortable. I saw Ate Liza sleeping in the back seat.

"How's your project with Today's Hope Faith?" Gabriel asked.

"Well, we still need two stories for the book. Aimee and I would try to write other stories." I replied.

"Oh I see, so what will you write?"

"I can't seem to find the right inspiration to write a story yet."

"I am sure it will come out soon."

"I hope so."

Finally, we arrived at the Youth Center. Thirty-five youth attended the activity. It was a mini-seminar about children's rights and how can they advocate for those rights.

The activity ended before 5 pm, Gabriel interviewed some participants while I checked on the photos I took during the activity. We helped to pack up the things. Since Ate Liza also lived in Laguna, she requested just to drop her off her house.

"Would you like to stay for dinner?" Ate Liza asked me and Gabriel before getting off the car.

"Thank you Ate Liza, but we should keep going," replied Gabriel.

"I also agree with Ate Liza, it's getting late," I said.

"All right, I will not insist. But next time...you have to eat here." Ate Liza said.

"We'll looking forward to doing that Ate Liza," replied Gabriel.

"Okay, you two take care!"

"Bye Ate Liza!" Gabriel and I said.

"Gabriel you can drop me off the next bus station so you can go home. We have work tomorrow."

"No, I will drive you home."

"You don't have to. I can go home by myself." I insisted.

"It's okay Faith, don't worry."

"Are you sure?"

"I'm 100% sure."

We continued on our travel.

"So, you already got some inspiration to write your story?" Gabriel suddenly asked.

"I will try to do it when I got home, so we better hurry."

"All right but before that, I'll try to help you get some inspiration!"

"What do you mean?" I was confused.

"Just trust me."

Gabriel slowly drove the car to the small coffee shop on the other side of the street. He went down the car and before I knew it, he was already opening the car door beside me.

"Are you hungry Gabriel?" I seriously asked him.

"We can eat later if you want, but you have to see this first..." Gabriel offered his hand.

"All right, this must be good!' I threatened him. I almost forgot that he offered his hand.

As we walked toward the coffee shop, I couldn't help but noticed the trees that were perfectly planted on both sides of the pathway. Though there were lights along the way, there was a portion that wasn't lighted.

I was about to say something when a small light passed before me. I was surprised at first, but I realized that it was a firefly. As we continue to walk towards the coffee shop, I saw many fireflies as if lighting our way.

Gabriel was smiling as he watched me experience the joy of seeing those fireflies. The sight was just amazing. Gabriel took my hand as he led me to the other side of the pathway.

"Look, Faith, there are more fireflies here."

My hand got cold. I was not sure if because of the fireflies or because Gabriel held my hand.

"This is really nice Gabriel, thank you!" I took back my hand from him.

"I told you so, you'll get some inspiration here!"

"How do you discover this place?" I curiously asked him.

"Well, my sister and I used to go here..."

"Your sister must have really enjoyed this place."

"Of course, every time we go here we'd play and catch some fireflies. But the funny thing was I couldn't catch one. My sister would always catch one for me."

"That's so funny indeed!" I commented.

"She would always joke that I'm just chasing fireflies."

"It's a pity. Have you tried to catch fireflies again?"

"I dare not because I feel like these fireflies would die on my hands."

"Would you like to try again now?" I gently asked him.

Gabriel looked so hesitant. His reaction was a big no. Actually, I was also afraid to catch one because we have the same fear. I always thought that fireflies were so sensitive.

Gabriel was just walking behind me. And finally, I caught a firefly! I hid my hand with the firefly at my back.

"Gabriel, meet your new friend!" I opened my hand and he saw the little firefly.

"It's so beautiful Faith!' Gabriel said.

He was like a child filled with so much joy. He was holding my hands as I let go of the firefly.

We continued walking until we reached the coffee shop.

"We are here. Ms. Katherine Faith Perez. Welcome to the best coffee shop in the world!" Gabriel said when we got in.

We both laughed. But I could agree with Gabriel. The ambiance was so great. Gabriel seemed to have so many memories here.

"Welcome Sir Gabriel, welcome Ma'am!" The young lady greeted us as she led us to a table near the window.

"Thank you very much," I replied. She sweetly smiled as she gave us the menu.

"Sir Gabriel, looks like you need some inspiration again, that's why you're here?" The young lady said.

"Well, not me this time," Gabriel answered as he turned to me.

"What can I say? I guess I already found one." I confessed.

CHAPTER 11

Doesn't Need A Reason

"What would you do to make the world a better place?" Pastor Nathan, our retreat speaker asked.

"Whatever your profession, condition or status in life, you can make a difference in this world. Looking at Jesus as the ultimate model in living would move us to follow Him. Jesus' radical discipleship, the ministry of reconciliation, the ministry of healing and looking after the poor are great models," Pastor Nathan continued his message.

The message was about a woman bleeding for 12 years (Luke 8:40-56). The story showed what holistic transformation was all about. The woman was healed physically, emotionally, socially, economically and spiritually. She was restored to health from her bleeding just by touching the garment of Jesus. She was also healed emotionally when the Lord Jesus accepted her and gave her importance by asking who touched Him. During those times, it was ceremonially unclean to associate with women suffering from their period, more so with a woman bleeding for 12 years. She must have suffered so much indignity in the eyes of the people. Jesus gave her the opportunity to regain her self-worth and dignity.

Jesus brought back her social relationship by letting her come out in front of all the people not just to admit that she was the one who touched Him but to unveil that her long time sickness was gone. Her social status was restored when Jesus said, "Daughter, be of good cheer; your faith has made you well. Go in peace."(Luke 8:48 NKJV).

She was also freed economically because at last she would no longer need to look and pay the physicians to heal her. In the story, she spent all her money to the physicians but to no avail. She could then start anew.

Spiritually, she was restored when the Lord Jesus said, "Go in peace." Her bleeding for 12 years held her from worshiping in the synagogue because people considered her "unclean." Reconciliation has taken place between the woman and God. He transformed the whole being of the woman.

The theme of the organization's retreat was "Restoring and Transforming Lives" and the message of Pastor Nathan perfectly explained it.

"As we start this three-day retreat, let us be reminded of God's love for each and everyone of us. We're here because of God's grace and love. God can restore and transform lives," Pastor Nathan concluded.

Pastor Nathan uttered a closing praying. The retreat committee was assigned in the response song on the first day. But I was surprised when Gabriel's voice suddenly filled the session hall as he started to sing "Amazing Grace." I thought Sir Lane would sing the response song but instead, he played the guitar. Pam was on keyboards. Ma'am Anne and Ate Valerie were the backup singers.

Amazing grace, how sweet the sound that saved a wretch like me
I once was lost, but now I'm found, was blind, but now I see
'Twas grace that taught my heart to fear and grace my fears relieved..."

I didn't know that Gabriel could sing. And he sang pretty well, I must say. The morning devotion ended. We needed to check in our assigned rooms. The session would resume in the afternoon.

"Come on Faith, let's go," Pam said as she carried her things.

"Go ahead Pam, I'll just follow you in a minute," I responded while waiting for the laptop to shut down. I was assigned to the multimedia.

"I'll get our room key at the reception, I'll wait for you there..." Pam hurriedly said.

I just nodded as I put the laptop inside my bag. I decided to get a glass of cold water first before proceeding to the reception.

As I was about to return to get my things, I was startled that Gabriel was just behind me. I was still holding the pitcher of cold water.

"You scared me," I said.

"Oh, I'm sorry. I was just about to get some water."

"I see. Here, let me help you." I pulled another glass and poured some water.

"Thank you, Faith," Gabriel said as I handed to him the glass of water.

I finished drinking my water and get my things.

"I'll take care of this..." Gabriel already carried by blue backpack and laptop bag.

"No Gabriel, I can do that. You don't have to..." I resisted as I tried to get my bags from him.

But Gabriel was just too strong and I couldn't even pull back my bags.

"Mr. Gabriel de Vega, I am not that weak to carry those bags." I insisted.

"Of course, you're not weak Faith!"

"But why are you doing this?" I asked while trying to grab my backpack.

He didn't answer. He was determined to carry my things.

"Gabriel...please. Just give those to me," I pleaded.

"It's all right, the reception is just on the other side," he answered.

"Why are you like this? You don't have to help me all the time," I exclaimed carelessly.

Gabriel suddenly stopped walking.

"I don't need a reason to help you. I just want to do this," Gabriel explained.

"I still need to know why..." I insisted.

"Seriously Faith? I'm doing this because you're my friend," Gabriel said.

We finally reached the reception area and I saw Pam waiting on the sofa. Gabriel put down my things and left without saying a word.

"Thank you Gabriel. See you later!" Pam said as she threw a meaningful glance at me.

Gabriel smiled at Pam and went ahead. I saw him talking with Lane.

"What happened? Have I missed something?" Pam looked confused. I didn't dare to explain what happened.

"Come on Pam. We got some things to do." I said.

While inside our room, I couldn't help but think of what I said to Gabriel, I was not supposed to say that. He was just trying to help. I didn't have to ask for a reason at all. What was I thinking? Of course, I was his friend.

What else could be the reason?

CHAPTER 12

Puzzled

"Because you are my friend..." Those words were still resounding inside my head. If only I could bring back that moment...I would never dare to ask him. But I guess I just have to live with it. Anyways, I knew that it was no big deal with Gabriel. Of course, it was nothing.

"Faith, Ma'am Shelly is asking you if you want to join the puzzle game," I suddenly felt a hand touched my arm. It was Pam.

"What? I am already puzzled!" I responded.

"Oh, no. have you eaten your lunch Faith?" Pam burst into laughter.

"I did eat my lunch, Pam. Well, I guess I just missed my dose of coffee," I explained.

"Do I hear some coffee conversations?" Sir Lane came in.

"Sir Lane!" I almost shouted. I was glad he came so I could avoid Pam's inquiring look.

"Oops... I hear you right." We all laughed.

"Anyways, as I was saying, Faith, are you joining the puzzle game?" Pam repeated.

"I'm not good at solving puzzles Pam?" I replied.

"I am in already. And we still need two players," Pam retorted.

"Gabriel could join you. He's good at solving puzzles!" Sir Lane suggested.

"Speaking of Gabriel, where is he now?" Ma'am Shelly noticed.

"Yeah, where is he, Sir Lane?" Pam asked.

"Well, I really thought he's here. He came out first from our room..." Sir Lane said.

I discreetly stood up from my seat to escape from the conversation and find my way to get near the table with the brewed coffee. Just by hearing them mentioned the name of Gabriel suddenly gave me uneasiness. I didn't notice that my cup overflowed with coffee and the next thing I knew it was all over my hand. I was so careless.

"Are you all right Faith? That really hurts!" I didn't bother to turn my back as I get the tissue that was handed to me.

"I'm good. Thank you," I plainly uttered trying to hide my swollen hand.

"That must really hurt, let me see," Sir Lane stated as he tried to inspect my hands.

"Oh, Sir Lane, this is nothing," I replied.

"Are you sure? You look unwell," He added.

"Perhaps, I was just tired last night. I only had three hours of sleep. Needed to finish some things," I explained.

"I see. You're really working hard to finish your book project huh?" Sir Lane asked.

"Well, I'll take that positively," I answered back.

Sir Lane was just so kind to wait for me to return to Pam and Ma'am Shelly. As we were walking, the glass door of the session hall opened. Gabriel came in. He was wearing a sky-blue polo shirt and faded blue jeans. His hair was neatly brushed up. He was always smiling but not that time. He was serious and I couldn't help but recall our "little incident" that morning.

I became worried and I didn't notice that he was already standing in front of us. Contrary to what I was contemplating, it was a relief that he was not mad or something. He seemed not affected at all. I was just being paranoid. What a thought!

"Hello everyone, so are we ready for the puzzle game?" Gabriel joyfully started the conversation.

"I am so ready! How about you Faith?" Pam turned to me.

"Hmmm...Sir Lane agreed to join you instead. Go, Sir Lane!" I said.

"All right, as especially requested by Faith. It's a yes for me," Sir Lane said.

I almost hugged Sir Lane as I thanked him. I heaved a sigh of relief.

"Good afternoon everyone! I believed we are all ready for our first activity..." Pastor Nathan welcomed us.

"Yes, we are!" We all replied in unison.

"So let's begin. I have here the puzzle balls. Each member of the team must solve it. You will be timed, and the team who would be able to solve the puzzle with the shortest time wins!" Pastor Nathan expounded.

The staff was divided into four groups- the Program Team, Finance and Admin, HR and Communications Team, and Special Project Team. The players lined up. At the cue of Pastor Nathan, each player started to put the shapes on the puzzle ball. Everybody was standing on their feet and cheered for their team.

The Admin and Finance won in the first round while HR and Communications got the second round. And then the final round.

"Go Marie! You can do it!" The Admin and Finance Team shouted.

"You can do it, Gabriel! Go for the win!" Our team cheered up.

"Okay, at the count of three. One, two and three," Pastor Nathan signaled.

Everybody was shouting, laughing, and encouraging Marie and Gabriel. In the end, Marie finished just two seconds before Gabriel.

"What a game! And our winner is Admin and Finance Team! Congratulations!" Pastor Nathan announced.

"And of course, congratulations everyone for being such a good sport," Pastor Nathan further said.

Gabriel, Pam and Sir Lane returned back to our group.

"That was really close!" Sir Lane pretended to cry.

"It was. I told you I'm not that good at solving puzzles," Gabriel said.

"You're really good Gabriel, just two steps behind!" Pam bantered.

"Guess you're right!" Gabriel concluded.

I didn't say a word and just chose to listen to Pastor Nathan's next instruction. As I concentrated on the lessons from the activity, Pam signaled me to move two seats from where I was. I followed her without complaint and continued to write on my notes.

"Hi, Faith!" Gabriel greeted.

"Oh, Gabriel. You're here. Where's Pam?" I inquired.

"She transferred at the back so she would not get cold. She said it's warmer at that area." Gabriel expressed.

"Oh, I see..." I wanted to tell him that she should call Pam. It was getting warmer on this side of the session hall.

It was a good thing that Pastor Nathan made a lecture for the rest of the session. I didn't talk to Gabriel also because he was so focused on the lecture. We were given readings and were instructed to make reflections.

"Tonight after dinner, we'll meet again. Just be ready to share your reflections with your group," Pastor Nathan stated.

After the session, I hurriedly get my things and stood up to call for Pam.

"Pam, wait for me!" I shouted.

"Hey Faith..." I heard Gabriel from behind.

"Yes..." I hesitated to look back.

"You dropped your pen," Gabriel handed it to me.

"Oh, thank you! By the way, congratulations Gabriel!" I said.

"For what?" He asked.

"For the puzzle game, you're really good. And I'm proud of you! I am pretty sure that it will take me forever to solve that," I tried to joke.

"I don't believe you, Faith. I am sure you'll do it better than I," Gabriel contradicted.

"I doubt it. I bet it'll be forever for me to solve that."

"Well, I must say that you should give it a try." Gabriel insisted.

"I'm sure you'll get it," Gabriel encouragingly said.

"How sure are you now?" I challenged him.

"I am 101% sure because I know you. And you're my friend!" He tapped my shoulders.

I just nodded not knowing what else to say.

"You need to try it tonight! I'll see you. I'll wait until you solve it. Even if it takes forever!" He waved his hand as he said those words.

He seemed serious about it. I stood a little longer as I watched him leave the session hall.

Now, I am really puzzled inside.

CHAPTER 13

What I Really Want To Say

"Hi, Rachel! I'm glad you called..." I answered my phone as I was preparing to go out for the evening session.

"Yes, of course. How are you? Is everything okay? I got worried when you asked me to call," Rachel briefly stated.

"So sorry Rachel, I just want to hear your voice at this moment." I reasoned out.

"Is there something you want to tell me?" Her voice sounded worried.

"Actually, I just want to make sure that you'd come on the book launch. I know that you've been busy with your work. Just checking... Does Justin call you about the program?" I asked her.

"I will surely come Faith. Justin hasn't called yet. He's been busy... I think," Rachel replied.

"I see..." I was thinking of what else to say.

"Don't worry, I'll call him tonight regarding the program. I will coordinate also with Ma'am Carmen and Teacher Angelo. Would that give you peace of mind now?" Rachel asked me.

"Absolutely! Thank you so much, Rachel!" I almost shouted.

"So, what else are you thinking? This is so you..." Rachel knew me very well.

"Well, I am not really sure of what I am thinking right now," I confessed.

"Okay, I see. Would you like talk about it?"

"I am also not sure what to say?" I added.

"Oh, Katherine Faith. You have to loosen up a little. Don't overthink. Sometimes if you don't know what else to say or do, just hang a little. Your heart will surely know...."

"I'll do that..." I replied.

"All right, I'm just here. Just a text away," she assured me.

"Thank you, Rachel," I said as we ended our conversation.

Pam was waiting outside our room. We went back together to the session hall. We came a little early. The Admin and Finance staff were preparing for the praise and worship. Pastor Nathan was also there. After the praise and worship, Pastor Nathan led a short devotion. We were instructed to group ourselves so we could share our reflections on the assigned reading.

The reading was about a Samaritan who helped a man attacked and robbed. It was found in the book of Luke, "Then Jesus answered and said: "A certain man went down from Jerusalem to Jericho, and fell among thieves, who stripped him of his clothing, wounded him, and departed, leaving him half dead. Now by chance a certain priest came down that road. And when he saw him, he passed by on the other side. Likewise, a Levite, when he arrived at the place, came and looked, and passed by on the other side. But a certain Samaritan, as he journeyed, came where he was. And when he saw him, he had compassion. So he went to him and bandaged his wounds, pouring on oil and wine; and he set him on his own animal, brought him to an inn, and took care of him. On the next day, when he departed, he took out two denarii, gave them to the innkeeper, and said to him, 'Take care of him; and whatever more you spend, when I come again, I will repay you.' So which of these three do you think was neighbor to him who fell among the thieves?" And he said, "He who showed mercy on him." Then Jesus said to him, "Go and do likewise". (Luke 10:30-37 NKJV).

Our group read the passage and Ma'am Shelly asked if anyone would like to share his/her reflections. Before anyone could volunteer she suggested if we could start with the person on her right. And it was Gabriel.

"So, I guess you'll have to share first Gabriel?" Ma'am Shelly smiled at him.

"Okay. Well, for me the story is one example of serving the needs of people the way Jesus would. And I saw some important points on how to do it. First, we have to see the needs of people around us. Another is we ought to sympathize with people like what the Samaritan did for the man. It is also vital to seize every moment to help. And finally, we must be willing to spend whatever it takes to help others," Gabriel shared.

He could really express his thoughts naturally I told myself. I must agree that seizing every moment to help others was so vital. Everyone in our group shared their insights. After that, we had a short prayer.

Everyone was reminded about the schedules for the next day and Pastor Nathan thanked everyone for the participation and finally called it a night. Pam and I decided to stay a little longer in the session hall.

"I'll be good in 15 minutes Pam. I'll just need to check on some e-mails." I told her.

"Okay. No worries. Take your time," Pam replied.

I sent a message to Justin about the book launch and requested him to help Rachel in the program. I wondered where he was. I hoped that he was not out of the country. I also replied the e-mail of Ms. Mitch of AGM Publishing Company regarding the copies of the "More Than Fairy Tales" book. It would be out soon.

"What else am I missing out...?" I uttered. I needed some coffee to awaken my thoughts.

"Pam, would you like some coffee?"

"A big yes Faith, thank you..." she answered back.

I became extra careful on dispensing the coffee so I wouldn't get hurt again. I successfully manage to get the cups of coffee.

"One coffee for you and one for me..." I carefully served the coffee to Pam.

"Really appreciate it, Faith..." Pam sweetly held my hand.

"How about me?" I was startled when I heard Gabriel's voice.

I turned around and saw him holding a box of blueberry cheesecake.

"Where did you get those?" I asked him.

"I brought it with me...." he smiled.

"Wow, thank you, Gabriel. You're always in time." Pam gestured him to join us on the table.

"My pleasure, you're welcome Pam! So I am not two steps behind now!" Gabriel jested.

"Yes, you are! Just a minute, I'll get our plates," Pam hurriedly got up from her seat.

"Do you want me to get you coffee?" I turned to Gabriel.

"I'm fine Faith. Thank you," he said.

I continued browsing the net as I started to sip my coffee. My thoughts started to scatter. I wondered what happened to Pam. She was taking too long to come back.

"Faith, are you ready to try it now?" Gabriel asked.

My heart began to beat a little faster. I was not able to reply.

"What do you mean try?" I sounded confused.

"You already forgot? Our agreement about solving the puzzle?" He reminded me.

"Oh, I'm so sorry. I got lost." I could feel that my face turned red.

"Can we just do it tomorrow?" I asked. I was not really comfortable doing it...not at this moment.

"Nope! This is the perfect night for you to solve this," he said. He stood to get the puzzle ball placed on the box near the platform of the session hall.

If only I could tell him that solving that puzzle was not what I want to do.

"Where's Gabriel?" Pam came back with the plates and fork for the blueberry cheesecake.

"There he is, getting the puzzle ball..." I said.

"Oh, that.... he's really serious about that?" Pam laughed.

"Okay, friends, let's do this!" Gabriel was so excited.

"Okay, for the blueberry cheesecake! Go!" I shouted.

"I'll give you two minutes to solve this...."

"That's too long..." I kidded. Could I possibly do this, I thought to myself.

"Your time starts now..." He said.

I felt like a child trying so hard to solve it. It was not easy, actually. I tried it for the nth time. I was a hopeless case.

"I give up. I can't do this." I complained.

Pam and Gabriel were holding their laughter. I couldn't concentrate.

"I told you, I'm not good at it." I tried to convince them.

We all laughed.

"Let's try this again next time, I think you're just distracted now," Gabriel observed. Oh no, he knew that I was distracted.

"Perhaps, I'm just a little bit tired." I reasoned out.

"That's right..." Pam agreed with me. She handed me the blueberry cheesecake.

"Thank you, Pam. This is the best part!" I replied.

Pam also gave Gabriel a piece of the blueberry cheesecake.

"This is really good, where did you buy this Gabriel?" I asked him as I was staring at the last bite of my share.

"I made it..." He answered.

"Oh, that's so sweet," I said.

"He really is..." Pam said.

"I mean the cake is so sweet..." I cleared.

"Faith, you're so bitter!" They said in unison.

"Ha ha, got you both!" I said.

Pam started to pinch me. We decided to call it a night and walked back to our rooms. Gabriel offered to accompany us on our way back. As we were passing by the pathway, I couldn't help but noticed the beauty of the night sky. I stopped a little to relish the sight. Pam gestured that she'd go ahead.

"It's so amazing..." I exclaimed.

"Yes, it is." Gabriel agreed with me.

We both looked up at the night sky.

"And beautiful as well...." I heard Gabriel said.

I was sure he was referring to the night sky. Of course.

"Good night Gabriel..." I said.

I went ahead. As I turned back, I saw him standing still. I waved my hand,

"Good night Faith! See you tomorrow." He smiled as he waved back.

CHAPTER 14

Something's Real

I was awakened by the ray of light coming from the window of our room. Finally, I had a good night sleep. Oh my, I realized that it was almost 7 am. I hurriedly got up. I saw a note from Pam. She let me slept a little longer so I could rest some more. I checked on my cellphone and saw several missed call from Gabriel. Pam left her cellphone charging in our room.

I was not sure how I managed to get myself ready in less than 15 minutes. I rushed my way to the dining hall and then I saw Pam sitting on the table located at the middle of the hall. Pam immediately noticed me.

"There you are Faith... finally. Come let's eat..." Pam gladly said when she saw me.

"I'm so sorry. You should have eaten first..." I apologized.

"Nope, you're good, just one step behind!" Pam kidded.

We went to the buffet table. As we got our plates Pam remembered Gabriel.

"Faith, where's Gabriel. He said he'll come to you?" Pam whispered to me.

"Oh, I didn't know he's coming...." I replied.

As we try to look for Gabriel, the wooden door of the dining hall opened. It was Gabriel. He looked bothered until he saw us.

"My phone is on silent mode. That's why I didn't hear your calls..." I tried to explain even if he was not asking.

"That's fine. You're here...." Gabriel expressed as he let out a big smile.

I couldn't think of what else to say so I just nodded. I instantly concentrated on the dishes in front of us.

"I guess we have to hurry. The morning devotion will start in 15 minutes..." Pam reminded us.

I picked some rice, chicken adobo and scrambled egg. I returned to get my coffee. Pam and Gabriel also settled down on our table. We asked Gabriel to say a meal prayer.

We started to eat. Gabriel was sitting in front of me while Pam was on my side. We were given mango crepe for dessert after eating. Without a word, I ate the mango crepe in less than a minute.

"Would you like to have my share?" Gabriel offered.

He was gazing at me when I raised my head. All the while I tried to avoid his look. And I really wanted to get up from our table and run away. My uneasiness was becoming real and real...

"Oh, thank you, I like mango crepe. This is really good." I was shocked to what I just said so I was obligated to eat his share.

Pam almost threw up the water she was drinking while Gabriel finished his cappuccino.

After breakfast, we all proceeded to the session hall. The Program Team led the morning devotion. The message was about forgiveness and second chances. They shared John 8:4-11 NKJV, "Teacher, this woman was caught in adultery, in the very act. Now Moses, in the law, commanded us that such should be stoned. But what do You say?" This they said, testing Him, that they might have something of which to accuse Him. But Jesus stooped down and wrote on the ground with His finger, as though He did not hear. So when they continued asking Him, He raised Himself up and said to them, "He who is without sin among you, let him throw a stone at her first." And again He stooped down and wrote on the ground. Then those who heard it, being convicted by their conscience, went out one by one, beginning with the oldest even to the last. And Jesus was left alone, and the woman standing in the midst. When Jesus had raised Himself up and saw no one but the woman, He said to her, "Woman, where are those accusers of you? Has no one condemned you?"

She said, "No one, Lord." And Jesus said to her, "Neither do I condemn you; go and sin no more."

"Like the woman in the story, each of us has this second chance to live a better life pleasing to our Lord. Jesus has forgiven the woman from her sins. She was not condemned and indeed she moved on to live her new life... we are all like this woman...but God has forgiven us and let's all do our very best for the second chance we have now. Perhaps we can say that yes we had our second chance already, but we have a God of many chances...let's never forget that." Ate Lisa from the Program Unit shared.

It was one of the most encouraging and powerful messages I'd ever heard. After the devotion, team building activities were facilitated by Pastor Nathan. We were also given lectures on our roles in the community we are serving, how can we best serve them and help them reach their full potentials as individuals, community members and as a whole community. We had unstructured activities and rest periods in the afternoon. Some went swimming, others opted to go to the recreation hall while others just rested in their rooms.

As for me, I just wanted to rest. I went straight to our room with Pam. I tried to read the book I brought while Pam took a nap. We agreed to take a break and would go out after an hour. I focused on my reading. At last, I found my concentration...I reclined a little.

I found myself surrounded by white and yellow roses as I was following the blue butterflies. I was captured by the beauty of garden uncovered before my very eyes. I couldn't help myself but move closer to the roses and smelled them. There were also white, yellow, pink, red and orange daisies. I picked up a white daisy and put it behind my left ear. I walked a little more and rested on the wooden bench I saw. I laid back on the bench and enjoyed the beauty of the blue sky. I closed my eyes and just listened to the gentle sound of the wind as if singing the most beautiful music of all... I could live here, I thought...

"Katherine Faith..." said one familiar voice. I opened my eyes and I saw a hand waiting for me to hold...

"Faith...Pam..." Ate Valerie's voice was so loud as she knocked on the door of our room.

I realized that I slept while reading my book. It was only a dream.

Ate Valerie came in as I opened the door.

"Hi, Faith. I'm sorry, did I wake you up?" Ate Valerie asked.

"No, I'm okay Ate Valerie. You're just in time." I replied.

"Where's Pam?'

"I guess she's just in the restroom," I responded.

"Okay. Anyways, would you like to go to town? We're going to buy additional stuff for this evening." Ate Valerie said.

"Well, I think I'd like to go. Let's wait for Pam, she might go, too."

Pam just went out from the rest room.

"I heard you both. But I'm afraid I'd stay here and rest a little more. I have an upset stomach." Pam explained.

"Oh no, I'll stay with you, Pam!" I retorted.

"No, Faith. I'm fine. Just please buy me tiger balm..."

"Tiger balm?!" Ate Valerie and I wondered.

"Yes, tiger balm. I already have my medicines here. I just need that..." Pam grinned.

"Okay... are you sure you're going to be fine?" I asked her again.

"More than 100% sure! You go ahead," Pam assured me.

"If that's the case, we'll be back soon..." I told her.

"You take care Pam," Ate Valerie said.

"So, who's coming with us?" I inquired from Ate Valerie while walking to the parking lot.

"The Finance Unit, Ma'am Shelly and Gabriel," she replied.

We went to the nearby grocery store in the town. I separated from the group so I could go to the drug store for Pam's tiger balm. After buying the tiger balm, I returned at once.

"Is that you Kath?" I heard someone called me. Few people called me Kath. And don't tell me...I turned to see who was it.

"Daniel?"

"Yes, how are you, Kath?" Daniel asked.

"Well, I'm better than ever!" I answered.

"Why are you here?" He casually inquired.

"Company retreat..."

"How about you?"

"I'm going to meet a client...and I also drop by to buy something..." he explained.

"Oh, I see. It's nice to see you. I have to go now." I saw Ate Valerie lined up at the counter nearby.

"Ate Valerie!" I shouted.

Ate Valerie waved at me. I walked away from Daniel. It was so awkward. I had moved on a long time ago but guess I was not ready to see him like this.

"Hey..." Gabriel started to say something.

I looked at him and I was really holding the tears from my eyes.

"What happened?" He was trying to talk to me.

I didn't know what to say. Should I tell him that I accidentally came across the man who broke my heart 15 years ago? I moved on, but it was so weird to face him again at this moment. I didn't want to reminisce it. I was turning my back when Gabriel caught my hand.

"Faith..." He looked so concerned.

I wanted to run away from him. But unintentionally, I embraced him instead.

"I'm so sorry Gabriel…"

No, you're fine. I'm just here..."

"Thank you…" I said.

CHAPTER 15

If I Had A Time Machine

If I Only Knew

If I only knew
that it would be the last time I'd see you
I should have embraced your heart so tight.
I should have memorized the look of your face
I should have held your hands a little longer
So I could feel you forever
I should have listened closely when you speak
So I could never forget the sound of your breath
If I only knew
that you would not come back
I should have told you I love you...
A million times...
If only I could wipe away
all the tears in my eyes...
And forget all the memories we had
If only I could ask you to stay for another day
I would look into your eyes once again

If only I could understand... all the reasons behind
If only I could tell my heart to stop waiting for you
It should have been easier just to let go...
If only I could ask you for another chance
I should have told you that the day before you go...
I would choose to be with you if only I could...
But all that I could do now is just pray for you
May you always be comforted when you feel alone
May you always find courage when you feel afraid
May you find the love that is meant for you
A love that would never fail and forever hold you...
I will be contented now as I also wait
For the love that's also meant for me someday
For a hand to hold that will never let me go
For a hand that will hold mine like the way you do.

-Faith-

I found myself sitting in front of Gabriel in the Memory Coffee Shop. It was only three blocks away from the grocery store. I remembered Gabriel holding my hand as we walked away from that place. He told me that Ate Valerie and the Finance Unit would follow us when they finished. I just nodded. I didn't know what to say or rather I didn't want to speak at all.

Memory Coffee Shop?!? The name of the shop amused me. I wondered why it was named like this. Maybe the owner of this shop wanted the customers to make happy memories here so they'd keep coming back.

I noticed the quotes written on the wall.

"Memories are the key not to the past, but to the future."- Corrie Ten Boom.

"The best and most beautiful things in the world cannot be seen or even touched - they must be felt with the heart." - Hellen Keller

"We must let go of the life we have planned, so as to accept the one that is waiting for us." - Joseph Campbell

"Sometimes the heart sees what is invisible to the eye." - H.J. Brown Jr.

"Love isn't something you find. Love is something that finds you." - Loretta Young

I was still looking for other quotes that I almost forgot that I was with someone. But, of course, he was not just someone. I was with Gabriel.

"So who is he?" Gabriel asked suddenly.

"Someone from the past..." I replied trying to think of a better answer

"I see...he must have wished for a time machine!" Gabriel exclaimed meaningfully.

"Why?" I wondered.

"So, he could be in your present..." He looked me in my eyes.

"Gabriel..." I couldn't help but smile. He could really be funny at times. I thought.

"That's better now." He let out a smile.

"Thank you for just being there." I was trying to make myself comfortable.

"Don't mention it. That's what good friends do and I'm one of them, right? You can count on me, Faith." Gabriel said without a doubt.

I nodded to show him my appreciation.

In a while, the waiter served us the cappuccino, cafe latte, and chocolate cake.

"No blueberry cheesecake this time, Faith. They say it was sold out." Gabriel whispered.

"Oh, that's fine, thank you," I replied.

"I hope these would make you feel better."

"There's no need for this. Just you being there made me feel better." What did I just say? Did I really say that?

"Oh, that's good to hear..." Gabriel seemed happy.

"I mean I am okay now. Thank you." I wished that I could take back the words I mentioned.

"Faith....Gabriel..." I heard Ate Valerie as she approached us. The Finance Unit was just behind her.

"Ate Valerie..." Gabriel waved his hand.

We had a good chat and bonding moment in the Memory Coffee Shop. Guess, it was true, we did make a happy memory here. I would sure come back here in the future. Before we went out from the coffee shop, there was a memory wall just beside the door. The crew said that we could write something on a piece of paper and attached it to the wall. I was hesitant at first, but Ate Valerie was so persistent for us to do it.

We traveled back to the retreat venue.

After fixing the things we bought, Gabriel accompanied me up to the door of our assigned room.

"Gabriel...I just want to say that I really appreciate what you've done back there," I said.

"You're always welcome. You go inside. We still have activity later. Take some rest."

As I opened the door of our room, my heart and mind were battling to look back so I could watch him leave.

"Oh Faith, I forgot something..." I heard Gabriel from behind.

"Yes. What is it?" I asked.

"Here, you can share it with Pam. This would make you feel even better." Gabriel handed me the Cornetto ice cream.

"Thank you..." I said.

Could it be that Gabriel was thinking that I was actually eating sugar? He was giving me so much sweet things lately. I thought to myself.

Then I went inside our room, still wondering.

"How are you feeling now Pam?" I handed to her the tiger balm she requested.

"Much better now. What happened to your eyes?" she asked. I was avoiding her to see it.

"Oh, nothing. They got itchy on our way back. I should have worn my eyeglasses." I replied as we went inside our room.

As I was heating up water to make a coffee, random thoughts were flooding my mind. I should have stayed with Pam instead of going to town. That way, I could have avoided that encounter with Daniel. I shouldn't have that awkward moment with Gabriel. Also, I shouldn't be confused like this. Most especially I shouldn't be here wondering...

Perhaps Gabriel was right about the time machine. But I must say that if someone badly needed a time machine, it would be me not Daniel. But of course, there was no time machine. I could never go back to the past. I knew that I should live in the present and just hope for a better future. The past was over.

"Seriously Faith, you're eating ice cream with coffee?" Pam was amused.

"Yes, I am serious." I wanted to convince her to try it but I remembered her upset stomach.

"But for now, you can't try this Pam. We'll do this again when we get back to Manila." I added.

I finished my coffee and ice cream. It did make me feel a lot better. Thanks to Gabriel for thinking that I was eating sugar.

CHAPTER 16

You And I

"There is a God shaped vacuum in the heart of every person which cannot be filled by any created thing, but only by God, the Creator made known through Jesus." Blaise Pascal said this. At many points of our lives, one way or another we felt this emptiness inside our hearts. I felt this in my life. But when I came to know Jesus, everything has changed." Sir Joseph, our Finance Director shared during the evening devotion.

"Ecclesiastes 3:11 NKJV, 'He has made everything beautiful in its time. Also He has put eternity in their hearts, except that no one can find out the work that God does from beginning to end.' It was God who put eternity in our hearts, a hole that nobody can ever fill up but Him. With this, may we all be encouraged by God's everlasting love for all of us." Sir Joseph concluded.

It was the last night of our retreat. Being reminded of this truth that only our God can truly fill up the hole in a person's heart was more than enough to hold on to God's love. If I'd be given a chance to go back in the past, if I had a time machine, I knew where I would go now. It was when God filled up the empty hole in my heart. My heart will forever be whole in the hands of God.

That night was also the much awaited Fun Night for the staff. This had been a long tradition of the organization and this year's theme was all about fairy tales--- anything about "happily ever after."

Pam would like us to wear fairy costumes. She told me to bring my floor-length chiffon royal blue dress and promised that she'd make me a small blue and white flower headdress to match it. For herself, she had her knee-length green dress matched with transparent fairy wings and silver sandals.

I was not good at things like these... wearing costumes, putting on make-up and the likes. Good thing, Pam was always on the rescue and her expertise was really awesome.

Admittedly, even if I got stressed on doing things like this, I really loved fairy tale stories...it would not be complete without saying... "and they lived happily ever after." In reality, I knew that not all stories would end in "happily ever after." But I was still a believer and a dreamer ever since...

Pam handed to me the headdress she made.

"For the fairy in the blue dress..." Pam sweetly said.

"Oh, thank you so much, Pam. You're the most creative friend I've ever known." I mused.

"Thank you for the compliment! Really appreciate it." Pam replied.

"Are you sure you're okay now?" I asked her.

"Actually, not totally...Faith, can I ask a favor?" She reached for my hands.

"What is it?" I suddenly felt nervous.

"Regarding our presentation, I think I couldn't do it. My stomach might get upset during the act." She really looked so worried.

"Okay, I'll try to ask Ma'am Shelly. Maybe, we can request to cancel our presentation. I'm sure she would understand..." I began to look for Ma'am Shelly.

"Hope that she'll agree with you," Pam replied.

"We can try, don't worry. Just stay right here..." I squeezed her hands to assure her that everything would be just fine.

I went out of the session hall to look for Ma'am Shelly. I remembered her saying that she would return to her room to get her costume. The Fun Night would soon start so I needed to hurry. I bumped into Sir Lane in the walkway.

"Sorry, Sir Lane. I didn't see you." I apologized.

"It's okay. Looking for someone?"

"Yes, I'm looking for Ma'am Shelly, have you seen her?"

"Ma'am Shelly just got out from their room, she should be in the session hall now..." Sir Lane recalled.

He was also in a hurry. I noticed the beautiful sunset from the other side of the walkway. I looked at my watch and concluded that I still got 10 minutes to see it. This could be a perfect sight indeed. Pam would surely forgive me if I just stay a little longer.

I was really fascinated by the beautiful sight I was seeing. I sat at the wooden bench nearby where I can clearly see the reflection of the setting sun in the waters. I didn't stay for long, so after a while, I ran my way back to the session hall. I forgot that I was wearing high-heeled sandals.

I almost fell down when the heel of my sandals was ripped off.

"Great, just perfect! At this time, really?" I said to myself.

I didn't want to return to our room to change. I took off my sandals and tried to remove the other heel. I've seen this before from a candy commercial. This must also work for me. But then no matter how I tried, the other heel didn't want to give up. I knew it, that commercial was not true. I laughed to myself. I had no choice but to walk barefooted until I'd reach the session hall. It was a good thing that Pam asked me to wear this floor-length dress. I was sure that people would not notice.

I was walking fast when someone called my name. It was Gabriel. Not again. Why was he always there when I have a mishap? As I turned to see him I was surprised at his costume. He was wearing a Peter Pan costume. I was really expecting that he would wear a Prince Charming or a Knight in Shining Armor costume. Well, I was wrong. Anyhow, he looked good at it. As a matter of fact, whatever he'd choose to wear, he would still look good. I couldn't help but smile.

"You're smiling at me..." Gabriel noticed my smile.

"No. I am not..." I denied.

Without a word, Gabriel came nearer and nearer to me. My heart was beating so fast. What was he trying to do? He reached for my hand. And I closed my eyes.

"Let me do this..." He grabbed my sandals that I was holding.

Then, he led me to sit on the bench near the infinity pool. I could also see the sunset from that point. He was able to remove the other heel of my sandals. He knelt down before me and put the sandals on my feet.

I didn't have the time to object. I decided to watch him silently.

"This pair really fits you well. You're good now!" He was still looking down and I couldn't help myself but stare at him.

"Ms. Katherine Faith Perez, shall we go now?" He looked straight into my eyes as he offered his hand to me.

"Well, what can I do? You saved this silly fairy in blue." I joked.

"Do you think, the silly fairy in blue would allow Peter Pan to fly with her?" Gabriel inquired.

"To where?" I asked in an absent-minded manner.

"To the happy ever after..." he stated.

I didn't know what to say. I was sure not if I heard him right. Was he rehearsing a line from the presentation?

"I'm afraid the silly fairy in blue forgot her wings..." I tried to answer him.

"Oh, that wouldn't be a problem." He retorted.

"Well, if Peter Pan has the pixie dust with him, the silly fairy in blue might reconsider," I said.

"Peter Pan will take that as a yes!" Gabriel expressed.

We walked back to the session hall still laughing with each other.

It was one of the best moments I had with Gabriel.

I just didn't realize that it would also be one of the last.

CHAPTER 17

The Waiting Never Ends

How can you hold on to something that wasn't meant for you from the beginning? This was a story of a young man who fell in love with a young lady who lived in a faraway land.

A young lady named Rhine was on the seashore watching the sunset when she saw a frail body of a young man lying on the sand. She hurriedly came to the man to see his condition. The man seemed to be breathing still she thought. As she put her ear near the nostril of the young man, she was taken aback when suddenly the man touched her arms. Good thing he was alive.

He slowly opened his eyes to see the young lady who was with her. He could see her eyes looking intently at him.

"Who are you?" The young man asked.

"I am Rhine. I saw you from afar. I thought that you were...Oh never mind, I'm glad you're alive," she explained.

"I am. At least for now..." The young man said.

"What do you mean?" Rhine wondered on what he said.

"If you will not lighten your grip on my chest, there's a big probability that I might have a shortage of breathing..." the man said almost laughing.

Rhine didn't realize that she was still feeling the chest of the young man.

"My apologies..." Rhine did remove her hands from the chest of the man and help him sit down.

"My deepest gratitude." John uttered when he was seated.

"My pleasure!" Rhine exclaimed.

"My name is John," said the young man.

They spent the whole time talking and laughing with each other. John was captured by the simplicity and grace of Rhine. Rhine also felt the same. It was like love at first sight for both of them. Every afternoon, they would wait for each other on the sea shore to watch the sunset. At times they'd build castles and collect seashells. But most of the time, they would just talk to each other as if it would never end.

Then one afternoon, John was waiting for Rhine. While waiting he started to make sand castles and collected some seashells for Rhine. He also collected dried woods so they can make bonfire when Rhine comes.

"John..." Rhine called him.

"Rhine, finally you're here," John replied.

"I am here. I will always come to you," she said reassuringly.

They sat to watch the beauty of the sunset. Rhine closed her eyes.

"Rhine, wake up." John was holding her hand.

"I am awake..." Rhine softly answered.

Days passed, John waited for Rhine on the sea shore. He made a sand castle and collected some sea shells. He also gathered some dried woods for their bonfire. He waited patiently for Rhine.

But Rhine never came back. Days and nights still passed. John decided to come again in the seashore where he could remember Rhine. He started to build a sand castle and collected some sea shells. He was starting to light the bonfire when a man approached him. The man seemed to come from the king's palace.

"Are you John?" The man asked.

"I am Sir," he replied.

"Princess Rhine wanted you to have this." The man gave him a small bottle.

"Princess Rhine?" John was surprised.

"My daughter said she dreamed of you to walk on the shore," the King said. Tears were starting to fall from his eyes.

The King opened the bottle and pour out the crystal clear liquid on the right leg of John. John slowly tried to stand up without his crutches. He tried to walk on the seashore.

"You can walk now," the King said.

"Your Majesty, thank you. Where is your daughter?" John asked.

"She's in the palace," replied the King.

John went to the palace. He saw Princess Rhine in the garden. She was sitting on a wooden bench. John slowly came near her.

"Your Majesty, is that you?" Princess Rhine asked.

"It is I, John," John replied.

Princess Rhine didn't know what to say or do. She didn't want John to see her like that.

John sat beside Princess Rhine and embraced her.

"Why do you have to give up your sight for me?"

"Because I love you. And I want to have my last dance with you." Princess Rhine said.

They spend the whole night dancing. It seemed unending for both of them. John could no longer hold back the tears from his eyes when Princess Rhine's body fell down. He thought that it would be the last time for them... their last chance...their last dance.

After some time, John went back to the seashore to watch the sunset. He lied down on the sand and closed his eyes. He was thinking of the good memories he had with Princess Rhine.

"I thought we would never have a happy ending..." John said to Princess Rhine.

"Well, they said that 'true love doesn't have a happy ending because true love never ends.' What we have is true love, and it will never end John..." Princess Rhine gently whispered to him.

Princess Rhine's sight was restored through the true love's tears that came from John. Only true love's tears could redeem the sight of Princess Rhine when she exchanged it with the healing of John's legs.

They watched the sunset together, built sand castles, collected some seashells and danced under the night sky and the stars.

Finally, they lived happily ever after...

Aimee just read a story from the "More Than Fairy Tales" book. This was the most awaited launch of our special project for Today's Hope.

Gabriel was the one who wrote this story. He titled the story as "True Love's Tears."

I didn't have the courage to read it as planned. Rachel asked Aimee to read it instead. I was really glad she did that. Months had passed since I last saw Gabriel and I had no clue where he was and what really happened to him. Days after the retreat, Ma'am Shelly said that Gabriel resigned for an undisclosed reason. I tried to contact him but he never answered my calls.

I had to go to the restroom to hide the tears that were starting to fall from eyes after Aimee read the story. Does true love really never end? I was not that sure anymore. I still want to believe in it. I still want to hold on. I still want to hope... But how can I hold on? How can I still hope? I was not even sure if Gabriel also saw me the way I saw him. If he ever felt the same way, I did for him.

"Faith, aren't you done yet?" Rachel called on me as she knocked on the door of the rest room.

"Just a second..." I dried away my tears and washed my face.

"Are you sure you're okay?" Rachel asked me.

"I am. I have to..." I said.

"There you are. I've been looking for both of you." It was Justin.

"Hey guys, Ma'am Carmen said, the groundbreaking for the construction of the new building would start in a while," Aimee told us. She was just behind Justin.

We all went outside for the groundbreaking. Ms. Mitch and Sir Joseph of the AGM Publishing attended the event. DGN Construction Company representatives also came. DGN would be the one to construct the new building for the boys of Today's Hope. Ma'am Carmen, Teacher Angelo, all the staff and children looked so happy and excited. The children kept asking me if Gabriel would come and I just didn't know what to answer. Rachel was the one who explained patiently to the children.

The dreams of Today's Hope for their children would soon come to reality. As Ma'am Carmen thanked everyone, my heart seemed to break just by thinking that the dreams of the kids were at hand. It was all worth it. I couldn't hold back the tears from my eyes.

I remembered Gabriel when he was here to support the book proposal.

CHAPTER 18

Holding You

I stayed a little longer at Today's Hope after the book launch. Rachel, Justin and Aimee also stayed to help in the cleaning. I still hoped that Gabriel would come by. I was convincing myself that he would not allow this day to end without seeing the children of Today's Hope. This was also his dream and he also worked hard to make this a reality.

"Guys, I think we should go to the coffee shop after this. What you think?" Justin asked as he was stacking the chairs we used for the event.

"Yes, I think that's a good idea." Aimee quickly responded.

"I agree, too," Rachel said.

Then, it was my turn to agree.

"All right, I will also come...can't wait for my cappuccino and blueberry cheesecake." My heart was pricked when I mentioned the blueberry cheesecake.

I tried to hide the pain I was feeling. No sentimental thoughts this time.

Rachel and I went inside the center to help the staff in the kitchen.

Ms. Jasmine, the social worker of the center turned on the radio and listened to our favorite Christian Radio station. We were washing the dishes as we listen to a song of Brandon Heath.

"Love is not proud
Love does not boast

Love after all
Matters the most

Love does not run
Love does not hide
Love does not keep
Locked inside

Love is the river that flows through
Love never fails you

Love will sustain
Love will provide
Love will not cease
At the end of time…"

It was a great song about love. Love never fails. It was really comforting to know that love always hopes and always believes when you don't. But for how long? I knew that the answer was just right there in my heart. But I was not sure if this heart was still strong enough to hold…to still hope…

"Ate Faith…Ate Faith…" I felt someone tugging on my blouse. It was Irene. Irene was a six-year old orphan staying in the Girl's Home. The children of the Girls' Home of Today's Hope also came for the book launch. Aside from the Boys' Home, the center had another center for girls located in another town.

"Can I help?" Irene sweetly asked me.

"Hi Irene! Thank you but Ate can do this already. But we can play later outside. How would you like that?" I said as I winked at her.

Irene smiled and give me a high five.

"Okay, let's play later Ate Faith. Hurry up!" she said.

"Yes Irene, just wait for me outside." I said.

She went out and joined the other kids. Suddenly we heard the shouting of the children.

"Kuya Gabriel!" Everyone seemed so excited.

Gabriel came. Was this for real? I became uneasy. I wanted to see him but I didn't know how to talk to him or even say my greetings. The last time I checked he left without saying anything. He left without even saying goodbye. I reminded myself not to make the same mistakes again.

"Faith, Gabriel is here." Teacher Angelo said as he went out to greet him. Gabriel and Teacher Angelo became good friends when Gabriel started to volunteer as a teacher in Today's Hope.

"Yes, I heard that Teacher Angelo." I realized that I sounded so defensive.

I still tried to continue drying up the glasses and plates but the more I pretended to be okay, the more I felt so awkward.

"Rachel, I think I have to go first at the coffee shop now," I whispered to Rachel as I handed to her the clean plates that would be placed inside the cabinet.

"What? Are you sure you would not even greet Gabriel?" Rachel asked me.

"I don't know...I am not feeling well." And I was not yet ready to see him I said to myself.

"All right, if that's the case, I'm coming with you."

Rachel finished returning the other plates and glasses in the cabinet. Then, she got her shoulder bag.

"Thank you." I simply said as I prepared myself to go out. We finished the cleaning up in the kitchen just in time.

Rachel and I went outside. I saw Gabriel talking with the children and the staff of Today's Hope. Deep inside, I wanted to stay but I had no reasons to do that anymore. Or should I say I had no courage to ask him what really happened? I was afraid to know his reasons. I was afraid that he would see how hurt I was when he left without a word. I was afraid that he would see my true feelings for him. I was afraid to know that I meant nothing to him and that I was just his friend. Of course, I already knew that. The truth was it was really my fault. I let myself fall for him. I only had myself to blame.

"Time to go Faith...are you ready?" Rachel whispered as she got in her car.

"Yes, and there's no looking back," I said as I closed the passenger's seat door.

"I texted Aimee and Justin to meet us at the coffee shop." Rachel updated me.

"Oh, perfect!" I tried to let out a smile.

"Perfect indeed. But your smile isn't." Rachel was so sure as she said that.

"Well, at least I tried." This time I really smiled. I remembered Irene. She would be disappointed. I texted Ms. Jasmine to explain to Irene that we would just play next time.

"I wonder what really happened to Gabriel. He must have good reasons for his sudden disappearing act. Would you not try to at least talk to him?" Rachel asked me.

"For sure, he got good reasons. It's just that I would rather choose not to know. It doesn't matter to me now. Seeing him from afar is enough for me. And the important thing is that he still came. As for me, this must end today," I concluded.

"Is that what you really want to do?"

"This is the best thing to do Rachel."

"You're giving up without even trying?"

"I don't know...is it worth it?" I asked Rachel looking for an answer.

"You can do better than that Faith." Rachel challenged me.

Rachel was right. I could do better but not at that moment. As Rachel started the engine of her car, a gray car just came in. I remember the lady who just came out from the car, it was Isabel. She was also here. But why? For sure it was for Gabriel. In few minutes, I saw Gabriel walking towards Isabel. Isabel gave him a sweet hug.

I had to look away.

I was not sure if Rachel saw what I saw because she was focusing on getting out from the parking area.

"I am really glad we left..." I uttered.

"Sure, I feel the same Faith..." Rachel seconded as she held my hand.

Finally, we arrived at the coffee shop. I missed this place. We got our favorite spot. While waiting for the menu, my eyes caught the table near us. I remembered the time when I saw Gabriel in this same place with Isabel. I didn't bother to ask him who was Isabel. Maybe I just didn't want to hear who she really was in his life. But what I saw back in the parking lot of Today's Hope was enough to know who she really was in his life.

"Okay, let me see. I'll have Shepherd's pie and black coffee..." Rachel ordered.

"How about you Ma'am?" The waiter asked me.

"Black coffee and chocolate cake, please. Thank you." I answered.

"I thought you'll have the blueberry?" Rachel asked me.

"I change my mind?" I said to her.

"Okay Ma'am would that be all?" The waiter asked again.

"Yes, thank you," I replied.

"Faith, you really look sick. I think you have a fever." Rachel extended her hand to feel my forehead.

"I'm not sure. But you're right I feel like having a fever. But this would go away soon. Maybe because I didn't have a good sleep for the past days... so excited for the book launch," I explained.

"Have you taken any medicine yet?" Rachel asked me.

"None yet. I'll buy some on our way home..." I said.

"Okay...we'll do that. I'll just go the ladies' room Faith."

"All right."

I looked at the beautiful scenery outside the window. The sun was starting to settle down. This never ceases to amaze me.

Rachel's phone rang. It was Justin.

"Hello Rachel, we'll be there in 15 minutes. Leaving the center now..." Justin uttered very fast.

"Oh, we'll see you, Justin. This is Faith..." I mused.

"I'm sorry Faith. Where's Rachel?" Justin asked.

"Just around the corner. Oh, here she is..." I handed the phone to Rachel.

"I'll leave you first..." I whispered to Rachel as I headed to the ladies' room.

"Faith, wait..." I heard Rachel called from behind but I just looked back and continued walking.

I passed by the same table where I saw Gabriel and Isabel the first time when a proposal happened here. I wished he was here. But it was just a vain wish. I'd rather not see him, especially with Isabel. No, not again.

Rachel was right, I had fever already and my head started to ache. Though it was still tolerable. I could bear this. Of course, compared to the pain inside my heart, this was nothing. This would soon go away after taking medicines. I wished I could also buy a pain reliever for my swelling heart.

I looked at my reflection in the mirror inside the ladies' room. Admittedly, I looked really feverish. No wonder Rachel noticed.

As I was walking back to our table, I had to stop because my eyes started to grow dim. Then, I felt a warm fluid flowing from my nose. I got it covered with my hanky as I manage myself to sit on the chair near me. I closed my eyes to somehow ease the pain I was feeling. I stood up to continue walking but I was not able to control my balance. I didn't know what happened next.

"Faith, can you hear me?" I heard someone say.

I opened my eyes and I saw the face of Gabriel. He looked worried as he called my name. He was holding me in his arms.

I tried to reach out for his hand but the remaining strength I had wasn't enough.

"Just hold on Faith...I am here now..."

Was it really Gabriel? I just saw him with Isabel a while ago. I struggled a little when I thought of that.

Did he really have to show up every time I have things like this? And why would he even come when he had to leave again? As I thought of those things, if I could, I would run away from him. But I could barely move. I looked away as I close my eyes hoping that he would just go away.

But he didn't.

CHAPTER 19

Not Letting Go

I made a mistake when I walked away from Faith that day.

We went to the same university. She used to write for our university paper. I remember the first time I saw her. She was walking so fast to reach their office that she'd almost run. I was sitting on a bench under the tree in front of their office. I'd love to go to that area to find relief from the shade the tree was providing.

Every time Faith would go their office, I couldn't help but notice her. Several times our eyes would meet and she would just smile at me. I learned that her true name was Katherine Faith Perez when I got a copy of the school paper. I'd read the stories and poems she had written. It was a reflection of herself. Then there was this one poem entitled, "I Will Wait."

I made a reply to her poem entitled, "For the One Who Waits" and submitted it to their office anonymously. I had never done that before but I couldn't help myself but reply on her poem. I put it on the bulletin board outside their office and unexpectedly Faith answered back.

We'd exchanged poems and then one day she left a message asking if I would consider joining the school paper and that she was excited to meet me in person. I agreed to meet with her but I refused to join the paper because of my schedules. I had the courage to ask her if she would consider having coffee and a blueberry cheesecake. And she said she'd love to do that.

Finally, we'd be able to meet personally. Unfortunately, my father got a medical emergency the day we're supposed to meet. My mom and I rushed him to the hospital. When my father was stable already, I ran my way to the university to meet Faith. I was so excited. I saw her from afar. Fifteen more steps near her.

Unexpectedly, a man came from behind me carrying a bouquet of flowers. He passed by me and gave the flowers to Faith. She looked surprised but seemed happy. I had second thoughts if I would still come to her. I chose not to come because I didn't want to ruin that moment.

I walked away that day.

Since then, I didn't have the courage to come near her. At one time, I saw Faith still waiting on the same hour we're supposed to meet. I saw her posting a note labeled "From Someone Who's Still Waiting." But I never tried to answer her back.

I knew that I let go of that precious chance to know her more...I let go of that chance to tell her how much I appreciate and admire her. She left a special footprint in my heart. For so many years I tried to forget about her until we met again at the mission organization.

I thought I had moved on. But I thought wrong. During one of our devotions where everyone was giving encouragement and hugs, I found myself in front of her. I was afraid to hold her. As I felt her face on my shoulders as we embraced, my heart beat so fast that I had to let her go soon. It was then that I realized that she was still the one who captured my heart. But how can I say to her that I was the one who didn't come? I was the one who didn't take the remaining fifteen more steps to meet her? How can I tell her that I prayed and hoped for this moment to be near her?

I had my life away from her. But in my heart, she stayed. Just when I thought I'd have this chance to tell her everything, I needed to go away. Should I tell her? But that would be so unkind and unfair to her.

"The doctor said, she needed to rest for a day and she'll be discharged by tomorrow," Rachel informed me as she entered the hospital room.

"That would be good. Thank you, Rachel," I said.

"She's really a hard-headed. I told her to sleep but she's been working so hard for the book launch. But that's where her heart is. What can I do but to support her?"

"I'm sorry that I was not able to help her Rachel," I apologized.

"Oh, that's okay Gabriel. We helped her the best way we could and everything went well. It was a dream come true especially for the children of Today's Hope," she uttered as she sat beside the bed of Faith.

I didn't know what else to say.

"By the way, it would be good if you'll go home first Gabriel. Have some sleep. You've been here since last night. Justine and Aimee are coming. We can take care of our dear friend here..." Rachel stated.

"I'll stay until she wakes up," I said.

"But you also need to rest. I don't want another person to be confined here due to lack of sleep...that's too much for me to handle." Rachel smiled as she said that.

And Faith would not be happy to know that when she wakes up!" Rachel added.

"Thank you, Rachel. But please allow me to stay...even until this day," I pleaded.

"Why, are you going somewhere?" Rachel became worried.

"Yes, I'll have to go soon..." I admitted.

CHAPTER 20

The Day After

I felt my hand being held as I woke up. I was somehow disoriented finding myself in the hospital bed. Oh no, I remember what happened at the coffee shop. How could I forget the look of Gabriel as he called my name and told me to hold on?

If I could I would tell him that I was holding on really. I was even waiting for him. While he was away, I felt that same feeling I had years back when I was still in the university. Somebody promised to come but never showed up. I never met that person and wondered what really happened. But I never lose hope that someday, we'd have the chance to see each other. Inside my heart, that hope didn't die down.

But how could I say that when all I could recall was him being embraced by Isabel. I shouldn't hope to be with someone who belongs to someone else. I knew that Gabriel and I had nothing special really. And spending some awkward moments with each other would not count as such. I should have known better.

As I looked at my side, I saw Gabriel sleeping as he held my hand. I slowly tried to remove my hand from him trying not to wake him up. But before I could do that, he woke up already. I turned to the other side of the bed the moment I got my hand from him.

"You're awake..." He said as he stood up.

I didn't bother to answer him back instead I pretended not to hear him.

"Faith, are you okay now?" He transferred to the other side of the bed.

"Oh Gabriel, is that you? I'm perfectly fine." I pretended not to recognize him in an instant.

I was about to turn my back again when Gabriel hold my hand.

"Faith, I'm so sorry..." I heard him say.

Why was he saying sorry all of the sudden? I was about to say something when he embraced me. My heart started to beat so fast that I had to protest before Gabriel could hear it.

"Gabriel, it's all right...I'm good as ever...But if you'll not let me go, I might spend another day here." I kidded.

It was then he let me go. I had to smile. Silence came after that.

"Thank you, Gabriel, for being here. I am sorry for the bother. Isabel might be worried about you now and you should really go. I'll wait for Rachel..." I told him.

"Oh, yes. Rachel would be here soon." He replied.

"Does she know that you're here?" I asked him.

"Who?" Gabriel replied.

"Isabel...remember?" I reminded him.

"Yes, she knows that I am here. Why?"

"Oh, nothing just asking..." I said as I tried to be at ease.

The door opened and Rachel came in.

"Hey, I'm glad you're awake," she said as she got closer to me.

"Hi Rachel. Guess I'm ready to go home now..." I told her.

"Not so fast Faith...the doctor said that you can't go home yet for a couple of days until you're completely healed..." Rachel seriously explained.

"Completely healed from what?" I was clueless. Aside from a lack of sleep which I was fully aware of, I didn't have any sickness. It was then Rachel burst into laughter. I knew it.

"I got you!" she kidded.

"Rachel, funny indeed!" I could no longer hold my laughter.

"Well, I guess my patient doesn't need me anymore now." The doctor said as he came in.

"You're so right Doc Martin!" Rachel agreed.

"That's good news. Well, Faith, for now, you're good. Just promise me that you won't overworked," Doc Martin uttered.

"Thank you so much, Doc Martin. I'll do what you just said." I assured him.

"Oh great. I'll have to leave now. You take care. By the way, Gabriel, can I have a second with you please? Doc Martin told Gabriel.

"Of course Doc," Gabriel replied as he looked at me and Rachel.

"I'll be right back..." Gabriel said as he turned to us.

Rachel helped me to get ready as we waited for Gabriel. It took a little longer before he came back.

"Thank you, Rachel, for everything, I've been stubborn and it was really my fault..."

"No need to say sorry Faith. That's why I'm your friend, have you forgotten? You're like a sister to me...and don't worry I was not the one who carried you all the way here..." Rachel began to laugh.

"What do you mean?" I asked.

"Gabriel carried you," she revealed.

Rachel shared to me that it was still four blocks away from the hospital when the heavy traffic built up. Gabriel decided to get off from the car and carried me all the way to the emergency room.

"I can't believe he did that." I was really surprised by his actions.

"But you have to believe Faith. If you could only see the look on his face. He was so worried. This guy has something..." Rachel told me.

"I knew that. I was sure that Gabriel would do the same to anyone," I completed her statement.

"I'm here, everyone is ready to come home?" Gabriel asked us as he came inside the room.

"Yes, we are...everything is set. You're the only one missing..." Rachel glanced at me when she said that.

I nodded. Gabriel came nearer pushing a wheelchair.

"Oh, no need for that, I can still walk... remember I just passed out?" I assured him.

"Are you sure?" He intently looked at me.

"Hundred percent sure. I'm better than ever" I tried a joke. But he was serious.

"All right, shall we?" He offered his hand.

"Thank you, Gabriel." I uttered.

At that moment, I freely held out my hand to him. Perhaps it would not be unkind to hold his hand without hesitation at that very moment.

I knew it was only a make believe that Gabriel and I had something special. After this, we'd be back to our own lives. He only came back for the book launch, nothing more and nothing less.

So I would stop holding on the day after this.

Tomorrow, I would be wide-awake.

CHAPTER 21

The Waiting Soul

A borrowed time ended yesterday. I prayed and hoped for it to last a little longer but this was the day after. I was back from my make believe to reality.

Doc Martin advised me to take leave from work to regain my strength. I just didn't expect he'd recommend a three-day rest. Admittedly, I'd been so caught up in the schedules I had lately. My body gave up though my heart didn't.

On second thought, probably my heart also did. I'd been restless for quite some time. Beating the deadlines for the articles and reports needed in the field, following up the publisher of the coffee table book and much more. I was blessed and thankful that Rachel accepted my request to take over my work at Esther's Home while I was finishing the work for "More Than Fairy Tales" book. I missed Esther's Home.

I remembered my promise to DJ to play chess when I come back. It's been a while. And then Gellie, Ate Dina told me that she would have a farewell party soon. Gellie would be reintegrated to her mother. After staying for six months in the center.

Suddenly, my phone rang. It was Rachel.

"Hey, Faith. How are you feeling!" she asked.

"Hi, Rachel. Just fine. I was about to call you about Gellie?" I replied.

"Yes, Gellie would have her farewell party today. That's why I called. Do you think you can come? She's been asking for you..." Rachel told me.

"Yes, I will surely come. Thank you, Rachel." I couldn't hold back my excitement.

"Are you sure?" Rachel wasn't convinced if I could do it.

"I'm okay now," I assured her.

"Well, that's good news," she said.

"Indeed..."

"I'll pick you up at 5 pm?"

"It's okay Rachel, I can drive."

"No, I insist."

"But I'm sure can," I told her.

"No, just wait for me okay?" Rachel insisted. This was a battle that I couldn't win.

"All right, you're the boss. I'll wait for you at exactly 5 pm then?"

"Really now? I thought I'm the boss huh?" Rachel stated.

We both laughed and said our goodbyes.

Just when I put down the phone, my phone rang again.

"Hello, Mom?" I was hesitant at first.

"Hi, Faith! How are you? Dad and I are on our way home..." She said.

"I'm okay Mom."

"I'm so sorry, we're not there for you. I just read the messages of Justin and Rachel when we were in the city. But we'll see you soon..."

"No worries, nothing serious happened. I'm okay now. You don't have to worry..." I said.

"Glad to hear that..." Mom said.

"You both take care. I'm better than yesterday. I'll have to go..." I ended the call.

My parents were on the mission trip in Capas, Tarlac. And I didn't want to bother them with my condition. And I was really okay. Plus, a three-day leave was just so precious. Deep inside I was worried about the things I need to finish. But it was a blessing indeed, I'd be able to attend Gellie's farewell party. I could still remember the first time I saw her in Esther's Home and how she taught me how to hug (the right way). Gellie was abandoned by her mother in a certain place and never came back. She was referred to by the social service department to Esther's Home for proper case management. After some time, the center found Gellie's mother. With several things arranged and through the coordination of the local social service and parental capability assessment, the mother was able to comply with the requirements needed for the reintegration. Hopefully, she would really take good care of Gellie this time and she would not be found on the streets again.

I really wondered how could parents abandon or neglect their children? There must be some reasons and poverty was one of them. But still, I couldn't agree. I couldn't put my judgment on Gellie's Mom. Of course, abandoning a four-year old child was really unacceptable. And still reintegrating this child to her mom was giving me second thoughts. But she was still her mother and we just have to accept the assessment of the local social service.

Gellie is a precious child of God and we're putting our trust in God. He's in control of everything. And that would be a good reason for this reintegration. We're keeping our high hopes for Gellie and her Mom.

I sipped my cup of coffee. This would be a long wait for me. It was only 9:15 am. Rachel would come at 5 pm. What could I do? Well, I just remembered that I had some laundry and cleaning to do. I started to wash the dishes when the doorbell rang.

I ran to the gate and saw Aimee and Justin waiting.

"Oh, what are you two doing here?" I was clueless.

"Good morning Faith!" They greeted in unison.

"Good morning friends! So what's this all about?" I asked.

"We just want to be with you today. Can we come in?" Justin asked.

I almost forgot. I hurriedly opened the gate and let them in.

"So, what can we do for you now?" Justin casually asked.

"Well, I was really surprised by this. You two, have Rachel called you?" I asked again.

"Oh, we're really hurt already. We come here voluntarily to help you in any way..." Aimee pretended to be hurt.

"I agree." Justin crossed his arms.

"Oh my, are you really serious?" I said.

I looked at them and realized that they were really serious.

"All right, if that's the case. How about preparing for lunch? Anyone can cook adobo?" I looked at them intently.

"I'm the best cook in town!" Justin raised his hand.

"Okay, I guess, he's really the best cook in town. I'll settle in washing the dishes." Aimee uttered.

I did my laundry while Justin cooked and Aimee indeed washed the dishes. Then we had our special lunch. Rachel missed this little gathering.

"Okay, guys, I mean ladies, can we rest for a while?" Justin asked.

"We need to wash the dishes, Justin?" Aimee insisted.

"Oh, you're right!" Justin agreed.

"No, I can do it... you both go to the sala. I'll handle this," I said.

"Okay, I'll just do this Faith. You and Aimee go there fast before I change my mind!" Justin sweetly said.

"All right, you're really the best Justin!" Aimee hurriedly went to the sala.

"Thank you, Justin! So sweet!" I gestured a two-thumbs up to Justin.

"No problem, such a small thing." He winked and signaled me to just go on.

Aimee was holding the guitar as I sat beside her.

"I missed you playing the guitar Aimee. I remember our favorite song..." I said.

"Yeah, I remember that... 10,000 Reasons?" She asked me.

"Yes, that's it..." I came near her.

"Let me try..." Aimee started to play the guitar.

Justin just went in also.

"Justin, do you still remember our favorite song?" I asked him.

"Of course, who could ever forget that," he replied. He positioned to the keyboards.

Justin and Aimee started to play and I tried to sing. Even if I was a little bit out of tune...

"Bless the Lord oh, my soul
Oh my soul
Worship His Holy name
Sing like never before
Oh my soul
I'll worship Your Holy name

The sun comes up

It's a new day dawning
It's time to sing Your song again
Whatever may pass
And whatever lies before me
Let me be singing
When the evening comes..."

Just when we finished the song, the doorbell rang. Oh, I guess Rachel came early. It was a good thing though. She could still catch up with us before going to Esther's Home. My waiting was shortened I had to say.

"I got it, ladies..." Justin stood up to open the gate.

We waited for Rachel and Justin to come inside but it took a little longer so I decided to go out also.

"Hey, you two, please come inside," I said as I opened the door.

But I was surprised that it wasn't Rachel.

It was Isabel.

CHAPTER 22

Saying Goodbye

I t was always a blessing to witness the goodness of the Lord whenever I am with Esther's Home. And that afternoon was not an exception. The staff and children prepared a farewell party for Gellie. She would be reunited to her mother this week.

"Gellie, just never forget that we love you and that we are praying for you. You may not understand it now but when you grow up you will surely remember this. Be a good girl and don't forget to pray..." Ate Leah said to Gellie.

Gellie ran to Ate Leah and embraced her.

Ate Dina requested me to say something for Gellie but my eyes were drowned by tears. Saying goodbye was one thing I couldn't really overcome. I looked at Rachel instead and she understood. Ate Dina noticed it and gracefully asked Rachel.

"Gellie, I will surely miss you. We will all miss you. But you'll forever stay here in our hearts. You became a part of us. We love you. And always remember that God loves you so much," Rachel uttered.

Gellie smiled. Everybody took time to embrace her. After a while, we closed into prayer. I also approached Gellie and she gave me the best hug in the world.

"Ate Faith, thank you. You know how to hug already!" she whispered to me. I had to smile.

"Of course, you taught me how. You're a great teacher Gellie!" I said.

"Be a good girl and eat well. We love you Gellie," I told her.

"I love you Ate Faith…"

We all played outside after the farewell party. DJ reminded me to play chess. He won three times in our three rounds.

"Okay, DJ. You won again. But it's okay. Ate is not feeling well, that's why…" I kidded.

"Hahaha, maybe Ate…" DJ graciously agreed.

We laughed at each other. It was almost 7 pm. The children went inside their homes for dinner. Rachel and I also prepared to go home.

"So, do we have dinner outside?" she asked me.

"Yes, we do! Justin cooked a while ago but we finished everything…I'm so sorry Rachel." I apologized.

"That's perfectly fine Faith! You don't have to say sorry. Knowing Aimee and Justin…oh that's a given!" Rachel declared.

We said our goodbyes to Ate Dina.

"Faith, when will I see you again?" Ate Dina asked me as she put her arms on my shoulder.

"Soon…we'll see about that. I can't wait to return. And Ate Dina, I have something to give you."

I waited for Rachel to get her car. I pulled out the paper bag at the back seat and handed it to Ate Dina.

"As promised Ate Dina, here's your copy of the "More Than Fairy Tales" book…" I smiled at her.

"Oh, thank you so much. I've waited for this," said Ate Dina.

"Hope you'll be able to find this interesting and make you feel good somehow…."

"It will surely make me feel good. Thank you so much.

"You're welcome!"

I got inside the car of Rachel and waved at Ate Dina.

Rachel and I decided to have dinner at Chips and Chicken Diner's.

"I'll have chicken broccoli and a halo-halo. How about you Faith?"

"I will try chicken tofu rice and a halo-halo also." I said.

"Oh, that's weird. You're really ordering halo-halo? Let me remind you that it's cold!" Rachel teased me.

"Yes, I know that it's cold. That's mainly the point of me ordering it. I need to have some cool spirit here and thinking to do." I confirmed.

"I see. Have I missed something?" Rachel asked.

"Oh, no. Just for a change. I heard that halo-halo is the best here..." I explained.

"Okay, if you say so. You know that I'm just here for you..." Rachel reminded me.

"Of course, I know that. Thank you Rachel."

I knew that Rachel had so many things in her mind already. And I didn't want to add another worry to her. I was really surprised when I saw Isabel a while ago but I would like to handle this by myself.

All I knew about Isabel was that she's someone special to Gabriel. Nothing more and nothing less. But after our conversation, her words kept coming back to my mind.

Isabel opted not to come inside our house instead she requested for us to just sit down on the bench near our garden.

"Faith, can I ask you something?" Isabel started our conversation.

"Sure, Isabel, anything..."

"Thank you.... Faith do you have any special feelings for Gabriel?"

I was taken aback by her question.

"Oh, Gabriel is a good friend and he is indeed special," I said.

"I mean; do you think you'll like him more than just a friend?"

If only I could run away from that moment...

"Do I really need to answer that?"

"I need to know Faith..." she said.

"Isabel, I knew that you and Gabriel are together and I'm so sorry that I bothered him when I was in the hospital. But I'm sure that we're only friends...nothing special between us."

"We are not together Faith."

"But, I thought you and Gabriel are..." I was confused.

"I wish we are. But we're just friends," she said.

"I'm so sorry..."

"All my life, I've waited for him to notice me. But he didn't. I thought he finally did until he found the one he's been looking for a long time."

I could only hold her hands to let her know that I understood her.

"Thank you Faith...I shouldn't have come here." Isabel said.

"Oh no, it's okay. Does he know about this?"

"Not exactly," she replied.

I thought I already regained my strength but after hearing Isabel's confessions, I felt otherwise.

"Faith...the waiter is asking if you still want to order a drink?" I heard Rachel say.

"I'm so sorry. I'll have a soda please..."

"And... anything else?" Rachel waited for my response.

"Can I have a slice of strawberry cake, too?" I said.

"Of course, make it two, please," Rachel requested.

CHAPTER 23

A New Beginning

I found myself driving to the road going to the same coffee shop Gabriel and I went in Laguna. I recalled when Gabriel told me that whenever he needed some inspiration, he would go to this place. Maybe I was looking for one also.

I parked the car in the same spot where Gabriel did. I remembered the moment when Gabriel took my hand as we walked to the coffee shop. How could I ever forget the beautiful fireflies that lighted our way?

New Beginning Cafe. I noticed the sign post as I headed to the door of the shop. Oh, that was the name of the coffee shop. I didn't see that the first time I was here.

"Welcome to New Beginning Cafe!" a young man greeted me.

"Oh thank you very much..." I replied.

The young man ushered me to a seat near the window. It was a perfect place to view the beautiful trees surrounding the place. The sun was almost settling down and I was looking forward to seeing the fireflies that would come out (I do hope to see them again).

The young man gave me the menu. When I looked at his face, I couldn't help but gazed at him. I was sure that I met him somewhere before. He smiled at me.

"I know you..." I softly uttered.

"Ate Faith, it's me!" he exclaimed.

I was thinking so hard to remember him. It took me a while to recall everything.

"We met in the youth center, remember Ate?" The young man helped me to recollect.

"Oh, yes... is that really you?" It was Alex.

"It's me, Ate Faith. I'll never forget you Ate, you're the last person who interviewed me in the center," his voice was full of excitement.

I was doing research with the children in the youth center last year. Alex was one of the residents in the center waiting for the court's decision on his case. I remembered how he shared his experience when he and his friends tried to rob a bank. He was waiting in the tricycle that would serve as their getaway vehicle. But they were caught. He revealed that it was not the first time he did acts like that. Alex ran away from home when he was nine years old. He lived with his friends and became a drug runner. His mother tried to find him but he intentionally hid from her.

Alex confessed that he was angry with his father because of what he did to his sister. He said that it happened when his mother was in the hospital taking care of him. He blamed himself because he thought that it wouldn't have happened if he wasn't in the hospital. He was so angry with his father but he hated himself more.

When I was interviewing Alex, he disclosed that he came to know God personally while in the center. The encounter he had with God gave him a new hope. He told me that even the other children in the center were hopeful for a better future. And I believed that. I knew that God loves these children and He has plans for each one of them.

At that time, Alex was studying under Alternative Learning System. He was determined to pass the exam for him to pursue his dreams. He wanted to be a nurse someday.

"How are you really? When did you get out?" I couldn't wait for him to answer.

"I am getting better each day Ate. Just a month after your interview Ate, I took and passed the exam for ALS and I am a high school graduate now," Alex excitedly shared to me.

"Wow, thank you, Lord. I'm so proud of you Alex!"

He timidly smiled. Alex's case was already dismissed. I learned that he started to work with the New Beginning three months ago. I could no longer contain the joy I felt and I stood up to give him a hug.

"God has been so good Ate Faith," he whispered to me.

"All the time, He is really good Alex."

We were both holding our tears as we parted.

"Okay, Ate Faith. I think I have to take your orders now, or else I might lose my job..." Alex kidded.

"Sure Alex and I don't want that to happen."

"I agree, Ate Faith!"

"Okay, let me see..." I immediately browse the menu. I only planned to have a black coffee and a chocolate cake but I've changed my mind."

"Let me try your broccoli pesto pasta, a fruity scone, and a tea jello please," I ordered.

I noticed that I've been changing preferences so often. Well, I was in the New Beginning Cafe, there was nothing wrong on trying new things really. And perhaps I should really do that. I would try to do new things, become hopeful each day and to try to see things and situation in a new lens.

I knew that meeting Alex here was not an accident. God never changes and He never fails to give surprises. My love for this place grew even more. The quiet and private atmosphere seemed like a soothing medicine to a searching soul. The smell of the coffee and the freshly baked bread and cookies were just fascinating.

This was a perfect place to find not only an inspiration but a new hope as well. I just couldn't contain the joy in my heart. Gabriel was right about this place. Maybe the owner of this cafe didn't name this as New Beginning Cafe for no reason at all. But more than that I was reminded of the steadfast love of God that never ceases. God's love is indeed new everyday. As I waited for my order, I pulled out my small notebook and pen and started to write...

Unfailing Love

I always dreamt of one true love
I thought I found it at last
But like the other stories, it must end

99

Left my heart bruised and broken.
I don't know how can I make it through
Unending tears keep on falling
I just long to find the one true love
That'll forever hold me through this life
I'm searching still but it was all in vain
I've learned that I must not chase love again
Love will find its way back until it decided
To choose your heart and stay forever
I'm giving up until You come
You embraced again my heart
You held the tears flowing from my eyes
You touched my face with a gentle smile
Your mercy found me, You made me stand
You lifted my head, You held my hands
You took all my fears away,
Your unfailing love has found me again
I have searched for one true love
But you've given me an everlasting love
The greatest love no one can take away
Your unfailing love that will never end.
Father thank you for everything
For always waiting, for always believing
Let me hold on to this unfailing love
As I praise You Lord with all my heart.
-Faith-

Like Alex, if not for the goodness and love of God, I wouldn't experience a new beginning many years back. I was also picked up and given a new hope by God.

Alex served my orders. The smell of the broccoli pesto pasta was so good and the look of the fruity scone was just mouth-watering. And of course, I couldn't wait to taste the tea jello.

"Ate Faith, hope you'll like all of these. Just call me when you need something, okay?" he said.

"Can you stay with me here?" I asked.

"I would love to Ate. Maybe next time Ate Faith."

"Okay, when you're not on duty...promise me that we'll have a date?"

"I promise!" Alex even crossed his heart.

People started to come in and Alex had to attend to them. He waved his hand to me when he transferred to the other side of the coffee shop. I enjoyed the food and the tea jello was the best. I decided to take a walk outside so I could see the fireflies when they come out. I wondered if they would show up.

I was just a few steps outside when someone called me.

"Kath? Is that you?"

Could it be? My guess was right. Oh my, of all places why here?

The last time I saw him was during our retreat in Antipolo. Not again. Not on this time...there was no Ate Valerie I could call or a Gabriel I could run to...

"Daniel?"

"Kath, it's really you."

"Yes, it's me...." I replied.

"You know this place?"

"Oh, yeah, a friend highly recommended this place to me. But I am leaving now..." I hurriedly passed by him. It would not be a good idea if I'd allow myself to talk to him any longer.

"Kath...wait," Daniel called. I turned to answer him back. Daniel looked me in the eyes.

"Kath, can I ask you stay even just for this time?"

I was unsure but a part of my heart was pierced slightly when he called me Kath.

"Just please call me Faith instead?"

I smiled at him.

CHAPTER 24

Let's End Here

"I s it the book from..." I stared at the familiar book Daniel was carrying.

"Yes, this is the book from Today's Hope."

"How did you get that?"

"Oh, I got this from Ma'am Carmen."

"You know her?"

"Of course. We are the ones constructing the Boys' Home."

"The DGN Construction Company?"

"Yes. Remember when we accidentally met in Antipolo? I had a meeting with Ma'am Carmen and she shared to me about the project you're working on."

"Oh, really?" He didn't need to remind me of that day.

"I am so sorry, I was supposed to attend the book launch, but I needed to visit one of our project sites in Laguna."

"That's fine, you don't need to say sorry about that." In my mind, it was a relief that he didn't come.

"But are you really okay now? I heard that you were confined in the hospital?"

"I'm okay. Good as new. I'm coming back to work tomorrow," I told him.

"That's good news!"

"Yes indeed. So what's new with you?" I asked Daniel not knowing what else to say.

I must admit that it was not easy to sit in front of him, pretending that everything was okay and trying to be myself. Looking at him, somehow brought back the memories we had when it was still us. When I was young I often heard that "First love never dies," but I was still convincing myself until this day. Probably, for me, it was more like "True love never dies." Just a thought. But what if your first love is your true love? I also remember a saying that "If you love someone, set them free. If they come back they're yours; if they don't they never were."

I had to stop my thoughts. At this time really? Sure enough, I was a hopeless romantic. But I knew better now. Well perhaps, this what would happen if I entertain some memories from the past. Daniel was my past and I had decided to leave that past behind many years back.

Maybe, God has plans why he allowed us to meet again. Whatever it is, I'm trusting God everything. I remember His words from Ecclesiastes 3:1-15 NKJV

"To everything there is a season,
A time for every purpose under heaven:
A time to be born, And a time to die;
A time to plant, And a time to pluck *what is* planted;
A time to kill, And a time to heal;
A time to break down, And a time to build up;
A time to weep, And a time to laugh;
A time to mourn, And a time to dance;
A time to cast away stones, And a time to gather stones;
A time to embrace, And a time to refrain from embracing;
A time to gain, And a time to lose;
A time to keep, And a time to throw away;
A time to tear, And a time to sew;
A time to keep silence, And a time to speak;
A time to love, And a time to hate;
A time of war, And a time of peace."

Daniel and I never talked after he called me that day in the office. But

I never forget how it broke my heart to let him go when all I prayed for was for him to come back to me. I never tried to ask our common friends about him because I simply didn't want to know anything regarding Daniel. This maybe the right time for us to talk again.

I was startled when Daniel answered me.

"Well, I am focusing on my work now. By the way, Nanay asked me about you when I told her that you were having a book launch in Today's Hope."

"Oh, I do hope Nanay is doing well." I never thought that my heart could still feel the pain of the memories we had.

"She is doing well. And you remember, Crystal? My niece...you were her favorite."

"Yeah, how is she now?"

"She's taller than me now and she just passed the board exam for nurses," Daniel proudly narrated.

"That's so nice. Oh, we're that old already?" I laughed to release the tension inside me.

Daniel also laughed with me.

"Well, I am not that old..." He immediately denied the fact.

I had to stop laughing when Daniel looked at me seriously.

"Kath, I followed what you said about her. I tried very hard to remember the first time I fell in love with Annie but all I could remember was you. Our relationship didn't last. After that, I just focused on my work until I built the DGN Construction..."

I nodded as I processed what I was hearing. All these years, I thought they were still together.

"I looked for you and I heard that you got engaged," he added.

"It didn't push through. But it's okay. I am happy with what I am now. I hope you are also Daniel."

"Yes, I am."

"Well, we should be happy Daniel. And we have all the reasons to be happy."

"But if we could turn back, would you still accept me?" he asked unexpectedly.

I didn't respond to him. I didn't want to say anything that I might regret.

"But we couldn't turn it back..."

"I'm so sorry Kath. I was wrong when I let you go."

"No, Daniel. It was destined to happen. I wouldn't be here if not for that. It was God's plan for both us. I may have lost you but God found me."

He just listened.

"And look at you, you're so successful. And I'm proud of you. I always believe in you. Nanay's dream for you came true...Architect Daniel Narvaez." I sincerely reminded him.

"But I also have a dream that is yet to come true." I avoided to look him in the eyes.

Before, Daniel's eyes were the most beautiful ones for me.

"Don't tell you're thinking to shift your career...you need to finish building Boys' Home first!" I kidded.

"It's you."

"What?!" I wasn't sure if I heard him right.

"You are my dream that is yet to come true..."

Daniel reached for my hand. I was startled by his act but I didn't protest. Maybe I also wanted to know if I still feel something for him.

"You're always been my dream. I'm sorry that I was not able to stand for you. I was so confused then. I didn't want to drag you into my mess and I was full of hatred that time."

I felt that Daniel didn't tell me what was his real reason why he broke up with me. He only said that he had other plans and I was not part of it. Hearing those words were enough to pierce my heart.

I wanted to believe in every word he said but my heart has changed. I sincerely loved him before but I'd outgrown it already. My hand wasn't cold anymore when he held it and as I looked at him, all I could see was the face of Gabriel. I got back my hand from Daniel and stood up.

"Daniel, I think I have to go. It's getting late...and I forgot to bring my eyeglasses. I might have a hard time driving back."

"Kath, I'm sorry for asking you..."

"Thank you, Daniel. I have forgiven you in the past. And yes, I also waited for this time. I have waited for you to come back to me and say the things you just said. I believed that we'd have our second chance someday. You were also my dream. Remember when we agreed to become the best Nanay and Tatay?"

"I am here now Kath...let's make that dream a reality."

"But my heart has changed. I changed..."

Daniel came near and embraced me.

"I will wait for you Kath to give me another chance to make this work?" He whispered to me.

I slowly moved away from his embrace.

"Daniel, let's end here..." I turned away from him determined not to look back again.

I went out from the coffee shop. Tears came running from my eyes. I was walking very fast to reach my car when I noticed the fireflies that were lighting my way.

CHAPTER 25

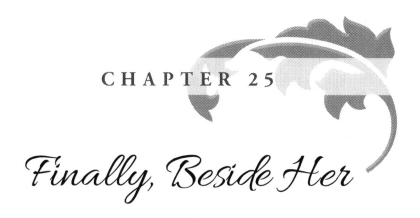

Finally, Beside Her

I opened the door of the New Beginning Cafe. I almost dropped the eyeglasses I was holding when I saw Faith being embraced by the same man she told me as someone from her past.

I immediately turned away and decided not to come inside. My heart was beating so fast that I could almost hear it. It was not a good idea to come here after all. I should have waited for her in the office tomorrow. When would I ever learn my lesson?

I looked at Faith's cat-eye shaped eyeglasses. I must give this to her. I accidentally put it in my pocket when we were in the hospital. I was sure Faith has another pair of eyeglasses but this one was her favorite. My feet slowly carried me in the pathway as I saw the lights of the fireflies. I remembered when Faith and I were walking here. She was so amazed and happy. I wished she could see them at this moment. I went to the other side. I tried to capture a firefly but I still couldn't catch one. I closed my eyes to feel the cold wind that somehow eased the pain I was feeling. I started to blame myself for walking away from her. This time, I would go back.

"Where are you? You said I'll find inspirations here..." I was sure that it was Faith's voice.

"Faith!? What's wrong?" I noticed her eyes. Is she crying?

When she saw me she turned her back and walked away.

"Faith, wait for a second." I tried to catch up with her.

"Sorry Gabriel, not now...I have to go." She headed to the direction of her car.

Faith really had a habit of walking and running away.

"Faith..."

"Gabriel, please, not now."

I knew that no words could possibly stop her.

I took her hand and held her tightly in my arms. I could clearly feel her heart beating so closely in mine.

"I am taking you home right now," I said as I wiped away the tears from her eyes.

Faith and I didn't talk along the way. I was glad that she fell asleep. She was still sleeping when we arrived at their home. I couldn't help myself but stare at her. The one I've been searching for so long was just beside me. I didn't wake her up so I could see her face a little longer. I really loved the way she sleeps so soundly. I wondered what happened to her back in the coffee shop.

I slowly touched her arms to wake her up.

"Faith, we're here..." I smiled when she opened her eyes.

"Oh my, Gabriel!" She was surprised to see me.

"You could at least say thank you, Faith?"

"I'm so sorry. Thank you very much." Faith hurriedly got out from the car and I followed her.

"How do we get here?" Faith asked me. She looked confused.

"We'll talk about that tomorrow Faith. For now, just go inside."

"All right..."

"And here's your eyeglasses..." I handed it to her.

"Thank you, Gabriel. By the way, how will you get home?"

"Don't worry about me. It's not that late, I'm sure I can still go home."

"Would you like to come inside. Have some coffee perhaps?"

"I'm fine. You go inside..."

"Is that you Faith?" A man and a woman in their late fifties came out.

"My Mom and Dad..." Faith told me.

"It's me."

"Dad, Mom this is Gabriel, my friend from the mission organization."

"Nice to meet you, Gabriel. Gabriel de Vega right?" Faith's Dad held out his hand.

"Yes, sir. I am Gabriel de Vega. Nice to meet you, too!" We shook hands.

"I read your stories, they were all nice," he said.

"Oh, thank you, Sir... it's because of Faith."

"And thank you for sending our Faith home. We really appreciate it," Faith's Mom said.

"Gabriel has to go home Mom, Dad..." Faith signaled me to leave.

"But, Gabriel would you like to stay for dinner?" Faith's Mom offered.

I thought it would be perfect if I stay but Faith winked at me. She wanted me to go home instead.

"He has to go Mom...right Gabriel?" Faith exclaimed.

"Yes, Ma'am. I really have to go..." I politely said.

"Okay, promise next time you'll join us. And I will not take no for an answer," she said.

Faith thanked me and I waved my hand as I left.

"Gabriel de Vega, how could you do this to me?" Sam bantered as I approached my car.

Sam waited for me in the gasoline station, a few blocks away from Faith's home. I was really glad he was in the coffee shop. He agreed to follow while I was driving Faith home. Sam was one of my friends in college. Just recently I learned that he was the co-owner of the New Beginning Cafe.

"Thank you, Sam." Sam went out from the car and transferred to the passenger's seat.

"You owe me big time Gab!"

"I owe you really, thank you."

"Oh no, I knew that look."

"What?"

"So, who is she?"

"Faith."

"You found her?"

"I did. Finally."

"And?"

"I don't know if this is the right time Sam."

"Well, if this is not the right time, when will it be?"

"She's with the same man I saw back in the university..."

"And?"

"They might be together again," I confessed.

"They might be? So, you're not yet sure?"

"Well, I am not sure. But I saw him embracing Faith."

"It doesn't mean that they are together."

"But what if they are?"

"Bro, don't make the same mistake again. Haven't you learned yet?"

I had to smile. Sam never changed. He was the same guy I knew then.

"Why are you smiling?" Sam asked.

"Well, I think you have a point."

"Of course, I have a point. Absolutely!"

"All right, I absolutely agree."

"If you really love her. Let her know. Isn't she worth fighting for?"

"More than enough to fight for... I wouldn't find her if she's not."

"Let her know. Don't walk away. If you do that, you may no longer find her in the next decade."

"How could I tell her?"

"Just simply tell her."

"Was it really that simple? But why can't I do it?"

"Do you really want to know why?" Sam was really something.

"Why?"

"Because you're so afraid. You're so afraid to love and to be hurt. But in the end, you're not only hurting yourself. You're also hurting the one you love...What if Faith feels the same way for you? What if she's been waiting for you also?"

"Remember Gabriel, perfect love casts out fear!" Sam reminded me.

Sam was right. I was really afraid to let her know. I had prayed for this to God and I should put my trust in Him.

I dropped off Sam in his house in Laguna and we agreed to meet again in his coffee shop.

"See you again Gabriel. I'll pray for you and Faith."

"Thank you, Sam!"

I finally found Faith.

And I will not walk away from her again.

CHAPTER 26

Road To Your Heart

"Good morning!" I excitedly greeted when I open the door of the Communications Room.

"Welcome back Faith!" Pam stood up and hugged me. "Are you sure you're okay now?"

"Yes, I am so okay..."

I headed to my table. My things were exactly where I left them aside from the small white box with purple ribbon.

"It's from Sir Lane..." Pam told me.

"Oh, really. Where's Sir Lane? I didn't see him at the HR Room?"

"He's in a seminar. He left that for you as comeback gift."

"Oh, he's so sweet," I said. I was about to text him when Ma'am Shelly came in.

"Good morning Ma'am Shelly!" Pam and I greeted her.

I noticed that Gabriel's table was a little bit different. There was a blue smiley pillow in the chair, the pens were placed in a gray cup turned into pen holder and a medium-sized red Starbucks mug on the side.

"Hi ladies! And I'm so glad you're here Faith!" Ma'am Shelly greeted us.

"Thank you Ma'am," I replied.

"I need a favor to ask from both of you? Someone must go to our Laguna Center to back up the new staff in the tutorial sessions of the elementary students." Pam and I looked at each other. From the look of Pam, I already knew what she meant.

"That's fine with me Ma'am. I can come," I volunteered.

"Are you sure Faith?"

"Yes, Ma'am!"

"If that's the case, you need to be ready in 30 minutes...Kuya Dello will drive you to the center. Thank you, Faith!" Ma'am Shelly walked to her place.

"All right Ma'am. I'll prepare my things."

"Thank you so much Faith." Pam winked at me.

We arrived at the Laguna Center in an hour. The session was about to start.

"Hi, Kuya Dello. Hi, Faith. I'm so glad you're here. You're just in time." Ate Liza welcomed us.

The Grade 3 students were already seated in their respective places. The teacher volunteers were with them also. I watched them comfortably at one corner of the hall. I started to look for our new staff.

"Ate Liza, may I ask where's the new staff?"

Ate Liza chuckled as she answered me.

"Our new staff?"

"Yes, Ate Liza..."

"He's over there with the kids. I asked him if he could do a storytelling with the smaller kids." She pointed to the direction of the new staff.

He waved his hand when our eyes meet. Even the kids greeted me when they saw me. He immediately proceeded to his activity with the kids. It was Gabriel. He didn't tell me last night about this.

I took some pictures of the teachers and kids during the sessions. Most of the time I couldn't help but look at Gabriel. I still couldn't believe that he returned. This session was for reading while for the smaller kids, storytelling session was being done. I observed and listened to the teachers. One of the kids from the group of Gabriel led me to sit beside him while listening to Gabriel. I wasn't able to protest

"Okay kids, I have a new story for you all today. This story is written by a very special person whose heart for children is so BIG... Are you ready to, listen to Kuya?"

The kids were laughing as they saw Gabriel making faces and changing his voice. He even tried to open his eyes so wide but he just couldn't. All I could see was his twinkling and smiling eyes.

"Yes, Kuya Gabriel!" The children shouted in unison.

"Okay...here it goes..."

Gabriel took out the book he was hiding from his back.

"Long time ago, in a faraway kingdom of Perpetuum, there were three princes living in the palace. Princes Fidem, Esperer, and Amare. Everyday after their lessons, they would come to the garden to play. They were so happy though at times they would also have little fights. They promised to be together forever. Until one day, there was a royal announcement that a strong storm would be coming and everyone was advised to be at the safest place. The king ordered for the people to take refuge inside the place.

The rain started to fall that night. Little by little it became stronger. The three princes were so scared that they would not leave the Queen. At the top of the castle, they could hear the roaring thunder and the heavy rainfall. Little they did know that the whole kingdom was already taken by the big water. Flood was all over the kingdom until it reached the palace. The three princes were separated, the King and Queen's bodies were recovered. Prince Amare the youngest was found beside the King. They thought he would die but he survived. Almost half of the people in the kingdom was taken away by the great flood. The King's men searched for the two other princes, Prince Fidem and Prince Esperer but with no success. Prince Amare at his young age was left alone and mourned for the King and Queen. He looked for his brothers with the help of a King's knight named Fidele. Fidele and the King's men helped Prince Amare to rebuild the palace.

Thirty years had passed but Prince Amare didn't give up searching for his brothers. He was still waiting for them to come back as promised. He remembered during the storm, the King told him to just hold on the piece of wood. He said he would come to save his brothers. Prince Amare was with the Queen but she was taken away by a strong current until she could no longer be seen by Prince Amare.

"I wished I was the one who didn't survive if I have to bear all this." He wept and the knight Fidele embraced Prince Amare. Fidele treated Prince Amare as his own son.

"God wanted you to survive my Prince. So you can rule this great kingdom and search for your brothers. Are you giving up now?"

"You know that I have waited and searched for them but my heart seems not to know which road to take anymore. Where could I find them? Are they dead already? It would have been easier if their bodies were found"

"Don't give up Prince Amare. Your heart will soon find the road to where they are..."

"We will sail to the next kingdom in our list and look for them." Prince Amare regained his determination. They sail on despite the storm coming.

"If I'll die here Fidele, please continue to find my brothers..." Prince Amare said.

He felt a hand grasped his to save him from the sinking ship.

Prince Amare finally woke up after three days. He opened his eyes and two familiar faces smiled at him.

"He's awake..." Prince Fidem said.

"Oh, my brothers." He stood up to embrace them.

The whole kingdom celebrated the coming of the two princes. The two princes were found by a couple in the country near the kingdom. They didn't remember what happened until the couple told them the truth. They chose to stay in the couple's custody and made them their family.

"We were sorry that we didn't come soon. But when you decided to go to the place where we are, we know that this is the right time...We are sorry we were so afraid to return to the palace..." Prince Fidem explained.

"We couldn't bear to think that our King and Queen were forever lost. I'm sorry my little brother. But there's no other road that we want to take but to be with you."

"I feel the same here... my beloved brothers."

Prince Amore broke down into tears.

"From now on, we'll stay together. Though it seems like a forever of searching and waiting, today is the day that I found the road that led me to you," Prince Amore told them.

The whole kingdom celebrated the coming back of the princes. And they lived happily ever after."

The children cheered loudly.

"Okay, kids. Do you like the story?" Gabriel asked them.

"Yes, Kuya," the kids shouted.

"So, what's the moral lesson of the story?"

"It's about the storm," one kid said.

"About Prince Amore!" said another kid.

"It's about happy endings," the kid beside me said.

I tried to avoid the look of Gabriel. But it was too late.

"Oh, maybe we can ask the author herself?"

The children looked at me. I didn't know what to say. But I regained my composure knowing the children were waiting for my answer. I cleared out my throat.

"Okay. I think it's about finding the road to the heart of a beloved!" I pretended to be thinking so hard for the kids.

The kids kept silent. I knew that I have to translate what I just said.

"That's perfect," Gabriel affirmed.

This day was another day to smile.

CHAPTER 27

Falling Rain

"Why are you here?" I asked Gabriel as I placed the learning materials in a box.

"It's a work assignment," he simply replied.

"I mean you didn't tell me last night that you'll be here..."

"Let's just say something has changed."

"Can I ask what is it?"

Gabriel didn't answer, instead, he quickly took the box from my hands and went straight to Ate Liza's office.

"Come on Faith, hurry up."

He kidded as he looked back to make sure that I was following him. I raised up my hands knowing I had no choice but to follow him.

Ate Liza was busy arranging the books on the shelf when we entered her office.

"There you are..." Ate Liza sighed.

"Where do I put this Ate Liza," Gabriel asked.

"Right there please..." She pointed to table near the bookshelf.

"By the way Faith, I guess you will have to ride with Gabriel," Ate Liza informed me.

"Kuya Dello left already?" I asked.

"Yeah. He's picking up some supplies for the medical mission tomorrow."

"Oh, that's fine Ate Liza..." Was it really fine? I had second thoughts.

"Will that be okay Gabriel?" She looked at Gabriel.

"Don't worry Ate Liza, that will not be a problem at all," Gabriel affirmed her.

"So, it's settled then. That's nice. Thank you so much."

I didn't protest. Well, I thought I still have so many questions to ask him.

Ate Liza would wait for her husband in the center. Before leaving, we helped her in arranging some books.

"See you when I see you!" Ate Liza said when we went out from the center.

"See you, Ate Liza," Gabriel and I replied.

When I realized that I was left with Gabriel, I pulled out the bottled water inside my bag. I had to restrain my heart before it'd beat so fast. I was drinking my water when I missed the last step of the wooden stair. I lost control and readied myself for some minor injuries. I got used to it, but Gabriel caught me. He was so close that I had to move quickly (but if he's the one who'll catch me, I don't mind missing every single step that will come my way). Stop right there, Katherine Faith! I scolded myself.

"I'm sorry Gabriel, so clumsy of me!"

"I know that...you're not wearing your glasses, that's why..."

"Oh...that's right. Thank you."

I did see that the laces of my shoes were untied. I sat down on the last step of the wooden stair to tie them up. Gabriel come nearer to help out but I told him that I could do it myself.

"Shall we?" Gabriel offered his hand to me but I hurriedly stood up. I didn't look back and directly went inside his car.

Though the traffic was so heavy, I wasn't able to ask Gabriel anything like what I thought of doing back in the center. Maybe, his presence was enough for me. I decided to make myself busy reading an online story entitled, "The One I Left Behind" by YellowPetals. Aimee was right, I got hooked by the story. She also recommended "Relentless" by Elydia Reyes.

It was almost 6 pm when we reached the Main Office.

"Thank you, Gabriel, for the ride."

"You're always welcome. I can drive you home if you're ready?"

"Thanks for the offer...but I have my car today."

"All right...maybe next time?"

"I'll check on Pam... Bye Gabriel." I immediately ran to the main door without waiting for his response.

"Hi Faith, I'm so glad to see you..." Marie greeted me when we met at the reception

"Hello, Marie! Is Pam still inside?"

"Pam left already. Ryan picked her up with the kids," she informed me.

"Okay, thank you. I'll just get my things. Aren't you going home yet?" I asked.

"I am. I'm just waiting for Sir Lane. There he is..."

"Hi Sir Lane, thanks for the comeback gift!"

"You're welcome Faith. Going home? You can ride with us..." Sir Lane responded.

"I'm good, you go ahead, I'll just get my things in a few minutes..."

"Okay, you take care Faith. We'll see you tomorrow."

Sir Lane and Marie left.

I was done packing up my things when Gabriel came in.

"Gabriel, you're still here?"

"Looks like it's going to rain Faith."

"I noticed that also. Let's go home. I mean, you should be on your way home by now."

"Yeah, I almost forgot to give you this..." Gabriel handed to me a box of blueberry cheesecake.

"Oh, what's this for?" I was hesitant to receive it.

"Well, I bought that from the New Beginning Cafe. I know you'll like this."

I was not sure on what to say.

"You don't like it?" He was worried.

"It's not like that...I just want to say that you don't have to give me things like this. I might get used to it. And I don't want that to happen."

"Katherine Faith, you're my friend. And..."

"And what? Then, you'll leave again without any words?"

"Faith..."

"Gabriel, can't you understand yet?"

"What is it?"

He seemed clueless. I looked straight into his eyes.

"Never mind..." I grabbed my backpack.

Gabriel got my laptop bag on the table.

"No, I can carry that!" I objected.

"Let me do this Faith." He was serious.

I felt like my face was turning red so I just let him do what he had to do. We reached the car park without saying any word. Gabriel put my laptop bag and the box of blueberry cheesecake inside my car. He signaled me to exit first the gate. He really got a beautiful smile. Katherine Faith, concentrate!

"Will I see you tomorrow?" I shouted to Gabriel as I opened the window of my car.

"Absolutely!" He smiled at me.

We parted ways.

I had so many questions for Gabriel inside my head. I wanted to ask him about Isabel. I wanted to know why he left and returned all of a sudden. I wanted to know who was the one he already found. I wanted to know why he was there at the New Beginning Cafe last night. I wanted to ask if he'll stay for good. I wanted to ask him why he looked so different now? Or was it only me that see him differently?

I pulled over my car at the bay side. I went down to feel the cool breeze of the wind. The wind was slowly blowing on my face. I closed my eyes and held up my hand...waiting for the rain to pour down.

"Lord, if he's not the one, please empty my heart like this falling rain..."

It was my prayer.

CHAPTER 28

I Will Wait

Two years ago, I decided to accept a new work assignment in Benguet. At first, my parents were hesitant, but they supported me. The mission organization set up a field office here and I really enjoyed working with the youth and the local people. I missed my work at Esther's Home but Rachel graciously accepted to take charge indefinitely. And I'm really happy to know that she's doing very well.

I still visit Today's Hope when I have time whenever I report to the main office. The Boy's Home was constructed already and I heard that the DGN Construction Company is now renovating the Girls' Home in Laguna. It surprised me that Daniel did what he planned. I remember him saying that he was praying to help in the reconstruction of the Girl's Home. I have to thank him when I have the chance.

"Hi, Faith. I'm so sorry I'm late," Thea said.

"Oh, you're just in time."

Thea's my friend since primary school. She transferred in Benguet a year before me. She told me that she fell in love with this place and with that she was convincing me to settle here. Surprisingly, the mission organization expanded its program to the youth of Benguet and here I am. And I thanked God, my adjustment could never been easier without this wonderful lady. And maybe, this is where I really meant to be.

Today Rachel will come to visit me. She said we'll just meet at the W.A Art Museum. At the museum, I noticed a new frame placed on a small table near the window. It was different. I knew this because almost everyday, Thea and I will pass by to go to the coffee shop located at the lower ground of the museum. Inside the wooden frame were two poems written side by side. I was familiar with the poems...

I Will Wait

You'd been leaving soon
And I don't know what to say
I wanted to hold you
Just for another day
The memories we shared
Will never be forgotten
Your smiles and laughter
Are here to linger
In my heart,
I wanted you to stay
But I understand
That you must go again
This is only for a while
That I know
Just promise me you'll come back
I will wait for you
Whenever you're alone
Just remember I'm just here
Standing still....
I am praying
May the Lord protect you
In everything you do...
May He always guide you
Wherever you may go
May you always be reminded
Of this love from above
As we wait for the moment
To embrace our hearts...

Ihrilyn D. Pendatun

For the One Who Waits

My love, I will remember
The memories we shared
Even though I will go
My heart will stay
If I had a choice
I will choose to stay
But I know you'll understand
I will be back again
Just promise me to hold on
As you wait for me
I'm praying for you
Every single day
I will remember
The smiles and laughter
The tears on your cheeks
I will dry away
May the Lord embrace you
When you are alone
May His love covers you
When you can't seem to go on
May you never forget
This love from above
As we wait for the moment
To embrace our hearts.
-Faith and Gabriel-

My heart pounded so fast. I could only hold on the frame close to my heart. So it was Gabriel. He was the one who never came. He was the one I waited. I looked around hoping to see him. All these years I wasn't able to recognize him. I wasn't able to see him.

I heard unending claps outside the museum. The poetry reading was about to start. Thea went down already to the coffee shop to grab her dose of coffee jelly. I tried to call Rachel but she was not answering the phone.

I hurriedly walked outside to find a good spot near the riverside to listen to the little girl who was about to give her piece.

Thea was waving her hand a few meters away from where I stood. I sat comfortably on the green Bermuda grass to hear the little girl. I closed my eyes to listen...

When We Dance

I don't know how to dance
How can I dance with you Lord?
I wonder how will it be?
Should I hold Your hand?
Or wait for You to hold mine?
I am so excited to know
How will it be?
I imagine myself making mistakes
And You are laughing with me.
What will be the music?
That we'll be dancing
Will it be fast or slow?
Ballet, swing or jazz?
I really wonder Lord
How will it be?
Until then, I'll wait here
Help me, Lord, to stand still
'Till You come and say
"Now, my child it's time to dance..."

The little girl bowed down. I knew that poem too. I've written that so many years ago. I stood up and when I turned back, Gabriel was there standing in front of me.

"So it's you?" I said.

"It's me, Faith..."

"You're the one I've been waiting...in the university?"

"I'm so sorry Faith, I was very wrong when I walked away from you and never returned. I saw you with Daniel and I assumed that you and he were..."

"I waited for you..."

"Not this time, not anymore," Gabriel uttered.

We walked to the other side of the river. The truth is, it doesn't matter to me now what happened in the past. It's enough to know that he is here. Two years ago, I prayed to God to empty my heart like the falling rain. It might be an answered prayer that the mission organization sent me here.

"How did you know that I am here?"

"That's a secret Faith."

Gabriel crossed his arms.

"Really now, you got some more explaining to do remember?"

I still don't know what would happen to us. Me and Gabriel.

"Are you leaving today?"

"No. I'll be here for three days. Ma'am Shelly said you need back up..."

"Liar, we don't have any activity to cover!"

We both laughed. I missed this.

"What about you Faith, how long will you stay here?"

"I need one more year."

"Oh, another year won't hurt...."

"What do you mean?"

"I had waited for you for almost two decades. Well, 365 days won't be that long," he said.

"Are you sure about that?"

My heart seemed to burst when Gabriel said those words.

"Yes, absolutely!" He held out his hand. For the first time in so many years, I freely gave my hand for him to hold.

We sat on the wooden bridge that connected the ends of the river.

"I'll wait for you here..." I heard him say.

CHAPTER 29

Holding Her Hands

"Love never fails" (1 Corinthians 13:8 NJKV).

She looked so different. Far different from the time I saw her standing at the bay side. Watching her from afar as she waited for the rain to fall in her hands brought sorrow in my heart. I knew that she just said her prayers as she closed her eyes, I could only pray that God would answer her prayers.

After a month, I learned that Faith volunteered to come here in Benguet. When I asked her reasons, she only told me that she needed to do this. If I could only tell her not to go, but who am I to do that? It was hard not to see her every single day, then weeks, months and even a year. At so many times, I would attempt to call her but it never happened. She wanted a space away from me and I must respect her decision. I remember a time when I secretly came here, she was teaching the youth. They were singing and dancing. She was laughing with them...I could tell that she was happy in this place. And that was all I had to know.

"Faith..."

"Yes, Gabriel..."

"Can I get my hand for a while?" I kidded. Since we sat at the wooden bridge while watching the blue sky, I didn't let go of her hand. Just by holding her hand gave me so much comfort and security that I really would not want to let it go.

The color of Faith's face slowly changed as she loosened her hold from my hand.

"Oh, I'm so sorry Gabriel de Vega!"

Then she crossed her arms. I pretended to be relieved as I stretched out my arms and slowly stood up. I held out my hands again to help Faith, but she ignored me. Holding myself to burst in laughter, I watched her as she walked away from me.

I followed her and caught her left hand, I led her to the end of the wooden bridge to see the blossoming white roses and yellow daisies. We silently listened to the sounds of the wind. Standing by her side like this was just so extraordinary for me.

"Faith, this day is our first love couple's fight!" I declared as I put her hand near my heart.

"Who says so? We're not even a couple?" Faith still looked upset.

"And you haven't courted me yet?" she added.

"Now, I am courting you..."

"That's so unfair!" She turned away from me.

"Is it?"

"It is! You didn't ask my permission!"

"Faith Katherine Perez..." This time I let go of her hand.

"Yes?" she replied.

"Faith...would you mind counting this as our first love couple's fight?"

She laughed. I didn't notice that tears were already falling from my eyes.

"Gabriel...I wouldn't mind at all," Faith said as she tenderly wiped away my tears.

"I should be the one doing that instead," I told her as I gently placed her hands on my shoulders.

"It's okay Gabriel, I'd love to do this. I'm sorry that I kept running away from you," she confessed.

"No Faith, it was me who didn't have the courage to tell you in the past the love I have here in my heart. I love you since then..."

"I understand Gabriel."

"And my love for you never stops..."

"You're here now and I love you, too."

God answered my long time prayer.

"Faith, thank you for letting me hold my hands..."

"And thank you for allowing me to choose you to hold your hand in mine," Faith replied as she embraced me.

I could almost hear the racing sound of my heartbeat as I embraced her back. Time seemed to stop and if it's possible, I would love to just stay like this for the rest of my life. She was my God-given miracle. The one I've prayed from above. She was the one whose hands I would forever hold.

"Thank you for choosing to love me unconditionally," I whispered to her.

We walked back to the coffee shop located at the lower ground of the museum. Inside the coffee shop, Rachel and Justin were already seated at one corner. Faith was so surprised when she saw them.

"Rachel! Justin! You're here..." she exclaimed as she came to them.

"Hi Faith!" Rachel and Justin replied.

"Could it be that you know about this?" Faith asked them as I approached their table.

"Nope, we're just here to visit you." They glanced at each other.

"I'm just so happy to see you. I miss you both."

"We miss you Faith, but someone really misses you more than us!" Rachel glimpsed at me.

Rachel led Faith to her seat as I get my gift for her.

"This is for you..." I handed a white box tied with purple ribbon.

"Oh, thank you, Gabriel..."

"Faith, remember when you asked me why I gave you the cake the last time?"

"Yes, I remember that. If I'm not mistaken, I didn't get any answer until now..."

"This is my answer..." I started to sing a song of Elliot Yamin.

"How do I get close
When she looks like an angel
A moment of her time just seems impossible to me
It's hard to find the words, to get to know this stranger
I'm scared of what she'll say if what I say sounds incomplete
And it feels like we belong together
Can someone tell me where do I start

Cuz, I can't keep on feelin' the way I do
I can't keep on, hiding my heart from you
I got to say something before
Someone else comes through,
I can't keep on loving you,
From a distance ...."

"Faith, thank you for waiting for me. I love you and I will not let you go this time. You are my miracle from God...will you agree that we really belong together?" I was holding my tears.

I put down my guitar and moved closer to her.

"Thank you for choosing not to let me go...for coming after me. You're my answered prayer. And yes, you and I belong together," she whispered as we embraced.

Love never fails.
(Artwork by Hanna San Jose)

CHAPTER 30

Holding His Hands

"Love suffers long and is kind; love does not envy; love does not parade itself, is not puffed up" (1 Corinthians 13:4 NKJV).

"I remember one meeting with my youth group. Our leader showed us pieces of pencils. Then she asked about our observation. The pencils have different colors. There were red, blue green, violet and so on. But one thing that caught my attention was that all of the pencils had no erasers. In my mind, pencils supposed to have erasers, so every time we make mistakes, we can correct them right away. But then again, those pencils were the special kind.

Just like the ordinary pencils with erasers, I was pretty sure that they needed to be sharpened, peeled off, and sometimes be broken so that the one who held them could use them well. Pencils could be sharpened in various ways. One can use the sharpener, the cutter, razor or even a knife. The processes they undergo were essential for them to be sharpened and used. Then after that, the pencils would be tested if they are ready for its special purpose.

They could be used in writing, in calculating, in writing beautiful songs, books, articles, drawing caricatures, designing houses and the likes. Nevertheless, no matter how sharp the pencils are, they will soon be sharpened again, undergo the same process so they will be useful again.

The outside appearance of the pencils will not really matter but what's inside of them.

While I was reflecting on that activity, I realized that we are like the pencils. The good thing is as we are sharpened everyday, we can be assured that this sharpening, no matter how painful it could be would soon lead to good results. We may not be able to write beautiful songs or even built houses but God has a purpose in His mind for each of us. We may be like the special kind of pencils or like the ordinary pencils, it will not matter with our handler, our Maker, Lord Jesus Christ, what matters is what's inside of us, our hearts.

We might think that we are just pencils with no erasers or maybe we are the pencils with erasers but just remember God can use you to start beautiful stories. God will definitely use us to touch people's lives." Jeremy concluded in his sharing.

Jeremy went down from the pulpit and headed to the row where Rachel and I were seated. Last week, he invited me to come to their church to attend their youth Sunday service.

Jeremy was one of the volunteers in the youth transformation program of the mission organization and also the youth pastor of the community church. Seeing him at the pulpit gave me so much hope for the youth here in Benguet. I felt so blessed that God led me here. I witnessed the hands and feet of God reaching and transforming the lives of many youths.

In the past, Jeremy attended a community diversion program. This was a program for children in conflict with the law or the children who committed crimes. When Jeremy was 15 years old, he was caught by the police using illegal drugs together with a man he barely knew. Jeremy was turned over to the social welfare service. And his life was changed forever.

He didn't escape the society's stigma of committing that mistake. But he was able to start anew with the support of his family and relatives. He managed to finish his studies and became a licensed engineer. When he heard about the new program for the youth he was the first one to volunteer. I could say that Jeremy's commitment inspired more volunteers and with that many youths participated in the program.

"Hi Jeremy, that's one big message...Praise God!" I whispered to him as he sat beside me.

"Praise God Faith," he answered.

"By the way, this is my good friend Rachel."

Rachel held out her hand.

"Finally, we met," Jeremy said.

"Nice to meet you, Jeremy," Rachel said, shaking Jeremy's hand.

The senior pastor asked the church to stand and led the church in closing prayer. After the service, Jeremy invited us to join him and the youth for lunch but I politely declined.

"Okay, Faith, I'll see you then tomorrow. Bye Rachel..." He waved his hand as he left with the youth.

"You take care Jeremy, see you tomorrow!" I said.

I was about to say something when I heard Justin's voice.

"Good morning guys!" Justin greeted as he approached us.

"Why are you here?" I couldn't hide my surprise.

"Good morning Faith! Hi, Rachel," Justin responded.

"Oh no, I'm so sorry Justin. I just didn't expect to see you here. I thought you were with Gabriel."

"Yes, I am. He's right there..." Justin waved his hand and Gabriel walked towards us.

Seeing him coming made me feel uneasy. I never expected that I would still feel this way. His face was serious but he really looked so nice with his round neck gray t-shirt and blue washed skinny fit jeans matched with his white sneakers.

"Hi, Gabriel!" greeted Rachel.

"Hello, Rachel. Hi, Faith," Gabriel warmly replied. Rachel elbowed me, I realized that I didn't greet him back.

"Oh, hello Gabriel. How long have you been here...with Justin?"

"Well, two hours, if my calculation is right..." he casually said.

If his calculation was right? Basically, he was here all this time. I automatically gave an inquiring look at Rachel but she just shook her head. Justin then grabbed Rachel's arms.

"Rachel, I'm so hungry, I didn't eat breakfast, would you mind having lunch with me?" Justin playfully said. Rachel punched his arms.

"Ouch! Now that really hurts friend!" Justin complained as he hid at my back.

"Okay, let's just have lunch together! Would that be fair enough with you guys?" I was holding my laughter.

"Fine!" Rachel and Justin agreed.

I looked at Gabriel.

"I completely agree with you Faith," Gabriel answered at once.

We had lunch at the nearby café. After that, Justin kept on begging Rachel to accompany him to the marketplace where he could buy some delicacies and souvenirs.

"Okay Justin, fine!" Rachel seemed pissed off already.

"You have to excuse us Faith... Gabriel, someone here is acting like a little brother to me. I'll text you when we're done..." Rachel explained to us.

"All right, you take care. We'll see you later," I reluctantly replied.

"We'll pick you up...just let me know where." Gabriel seconded.

"Thank you so much bro," Justin happily responded.

Gabriel and I watched them leave.

As we were waiting for our coffee, Gabriel handed me a blue scrapbook beautifully tied with silver strings.

"What is this?"

"Try to open it," he suggested.

I untied the strings and open the scrapbook. The first page was labeled, "Couple's Bucket List." Our names were written under it. I started to turn the next page...

1. Go to church together.
2. Stargazing date.
3. Hold hands.
4. Sing and dance together.
5. Say I love you when...
6. Finish a fairytale story.
7. Read old books together.
8. Mountain climbing.
9. Go biking.
10.. 11.. 12.. 13..14... and the list goes on...

"You really prepared this Gabriel?"

"What do you think?"

"You're like a child! Are you serious?"

"Oh, you don't like it?"

"I really love this Gabriel!"

"Really?! Yes!" He literally shouted.

My heart was rejoicing inside.

"Okay, where do you want to start?" I asked him trying to keep my calm.

"Well, please do the honor to choose Ms. Perez..."

"Okay Mr. De Vega, I'll choose number 3!"

"Number 3? We did that already Faith."

"Yeah, I knew that."

"Hmm... you might get tired of doing that?"

"I will never get tired...especially with you!"

Gabriel moved his chair beside me and offered his hand.

"Guess, I would rather stay here and not come back to Manila," he said as he gently squeezed my hand.

Holding his hand gave me so much comfort and love.

"Can I add some more to the list?" I excitedly asked him.

"Hmmm...I'll think about that..."

I tried to pull back my hand from him. But he never let go, I knew that he was teasing me. And the truth was, I was contented by just holding his hand.

"Okay, I will allow you with one condition?"

"Then, what is it?"

"I just have one question..."

"Go ahead, you can ask me anything..." I smiled at him.

"Why didn't you ask me to come with you this morning?"

Oh my, what should I say? I knew that I had no valid reason for not asking him. I was just so nervous to see him.

"Just because of...." I couldn't think of an excuse. Gabriel closely looked me in the eyes.

"The man who shared at the church?"

"Who? Jeremy?"

"Oh, that's his name..."

"Yeah, that's his name..."

"So, he's the reason why?"

"What? Oh, yes he's the reason..." I just let him be the reason. It was a lame excuse but I couldn't think anymore.

"Oh, really. So while I was thinking of you in Manila, you were so busy with Jeremy? That's so heartbreaking!"

"Oh, that's not heartbreaking. I'm sure Isabel is with you!"

"Isabel?" Gabriel was taken aback.

"Yes, Isabel, remember?"

"I got it, so you're jealous now?"

"Of course not!" I defended myself.

"Number 5!"

"And what is it this time?"

"Katherine Faith, I love you. And I will always say this whenever you're jealous," he said grinning.

I looked down at the blue scrapbook, then I understood what he wanted to say. Yesterday, Rachel asked me to describe the moment when Gabriel and I finally confessed to each other. I just couldn't answer and I wondered why. Now, I know the reason. And I thank God for everything and pray that this will not end.

CHAPTER 31

Shooting Stars

"Wait on the LORD; Be of good courage, And He shall strengthen your heart; Wait, I say, on the LORD!" (Psalm 27:14 NKJV).

Looking at the night sky, I remembered a moment when I was still young. It was Sunday evening when my parents and I went to the park. That was indeed a very special day for me. It was my birthday. We've been looking up to the sky while my Mom was telling her stories. I was hoping to see a shooting star that night. While listening to Mom, Dad and I were looking at the night sky. For a long time, we didn't see any shooting star, but then when I looked down for a second... there went the shooting star. I could only heave a sigh. I felt that I was deprived of something so beautiful, something I waited for a very long time.

I waited again and focused my eyes on the sky. I was hoping that I will see one this time. Then suddenly, I saw something. I thought it was a star, but then the star is moving and blinking. I looked at my Dad and said "Shooting star?!" We burst into laughter when we realized that it wasn't a shooting star after all, but an airplane passing by.

Will I ever see another shooting star? I said to myself. I waited. Maybe I was not just focusing, I should refocus, then just when the time I feel like looking down again. My Dad held my head up. I almost missed the shooting star. Finally, I saw it. We saw it together. There was an

indescribable joy in my heart... I was just so happy to see a shooting star and I couldn't explain why.

Whenever I look back on that day, I came to realize that the Lord has taught me a very important lesson from that experience. It reminded me of how I'd been walking with the Lord all these years. It has been so many years. There were ups and down. There were struggles, problems, tests, and trials. Through the faith that the Lord gave to me, I was able to stand up each time I fall. But there were also times that I wasn't able to stand up, and the Lord never failed to pick me up again.

I have made different decisions. Some of these decisions caused hurts and pains, which I could barely remember while some hurts I must admit visit occasionally in my heart. Nevertheless, I realized that the only decision I made for the Lord remained and stood. And every time I failed, what I couldn't forget was that the Lord always showed His favor and grace. He is always there ready to forgive and accept me again though I've hurt Him repeatedly. He has His ways of reminding me, as if saying, "My child, go on, get up, I'm still waiting, just focus on Me." God's love never fails and only Him can give that kind of love. I just need to look up.

Like the way I waited for the shooting star, I realized that at times while I've been waiting on the Lord instead of looking up to the Him, I looked down, hence I missed to see Him so many times. In a blink of an eye, I missed the shooting star like the way I missed the Lord God coming into my life.

I closed my eyes and uttered a prayer to God.

"You won't see a shooting star with your eyes closed Gabriel..." Faith was already standing in front of me when I opened my eyes. I was unable to say anything.

"How can you see the beautiful stars with that?" She stared closely at me.

She then grabbed my arms and led me to sit on top of my white 4 x 4 pick-up. I had to smile. Beside me was the woman I had prayed to be with to gaze the stars like this.

"Star light, star bright, first star I see tonight, wish I may wish I might have the wish I wish tonight..." Faith recited. I remembered repeating those lines when I was young.

"Do you really believe that your wish will be granted?" I curiously asked her.

"Well, I really don't mind. I'm doing the number 2! Stargazing date, remember?"

If I could only stop the time, I wouldn't travel back to Manila. Faith will stay here for another year but I'd make sure to visit her as often as I could. I was still hoping to see a shooting star before we say good bye.

"Gabriel, what are you thinking?"

"I'm thinking about my work back in Manila..."

Faith suddenly hit me in the arm.

"That hurts...is that how you'll send me off?" I complained.

"Actually, that's your fault!" We both laughed. I would surely miss her. Her face was turning red again and I really loved that look.

"Oh, look Gabriel, a shooting star!" Faith pointed to the night sky.

"Oh, I missed it, Faith!"

"No, you don't..." she said.

"Faith, I'm beginning to notice that..."

"And what have you notice?"

"That you're fond of picking on me...."

"I'm serious Gabriel and I already got it for you!" Faith pulled out a silver star-shaped box from her bag and handed it to me.

Inside the box was a couple's necklace, written on it...TO INFINITY & BEYOND. Faith quickly get the first part of the couple's necklace and put it on me. She then handed the other part to me and gestured me to put it on her.

"I should be the one giving this to you..." But Faith stopped me from speaking.

"Thank you Gabriel...this is the best stargazing date ever..."

"Yes, this is the best stargazing date ever!" I agreed.

"And happy birthday!"

"How did you know that?"

"Well, I have my ever reliable sources." Faith winked at me. And I rest my case.

I thanked God for allowing me to see the shooting star when I was a child and even allowing me to see Him in my life. I would still love to wait for a shooting star at night with Faith, of course. But I would no longer wait for a shooting star to make a wish but be reminded to focus on the Lord. I would continually thank Him for the shooting star and for this wonderful woman beside me.

CHAPTER 32

Immeasurable

"For I am persuaded that neither death nor life, nor angels nor principalities nor powers, nor things present nor things to come, nor height nor depth, nor any other created thing, shall be able to separate us from the love of God which is in Christ Jesus our Lord" (Romans 8:38-39 NKJV).

L et me call him Mang Andoy. He was 41 years old, married with five children. I only met him thrice, but those meetings left a footprint in my heart until now. He reminded me that nothing can really separate us from the Love of God...

Four months ago, our cluster leader instructed us to find a three-house Bible Study in the barangay we're assigned into. We were grouped into three's. My partners, Ate Marivic and Kuya Rolly. For a first timer, I was so excited and at the same time nervous to ask people in the streets if they like to open their house Bible Study for the Lord.

With the tracts, bible and with the instruction of our cluster leader- we went and followed. Our prayer--- for the Lord to lead us to his people whose hearts are ready. We knew that our work is not to convince the people but to tell them the Good News.

Then, we met Mang Andoy in the corner of the street of the barangay. with He was not really the one we're supposed to talk with but the woman beside him in their group. But after giving tracts and a short conversation, we ended up talking to him.

He agreed to pray the "prayer of acceptance." Ate Marivic led the prayer and as she said the words... "Lord, I confess that I am a sinner..." Mang Andoy protested and said," I cannot accept that..." But eventually ended up following the prayer.

Mang Andoy agreed to hold a Bible Study in their house for the following week. We were very happy we had our first house BS. We continued our search for two more. It was not easy. Rejections were unavoidable. But with God's help, we found another and then another.

The following week came, our first BS with Mang Andoy. My second meeting with him. The man we saw sitting on the corner of the street now sat on a small sofa. He explained that he was really sick because of hypertension. Her wife even told us that normally if Mang Andoy was sick, he would not allow anyone, to talk to him.

But we're very thankful, he accommodated us. Mang Andoy with his weak voice began to tell his life story. We learned that he was a former a gambling lord. There was a moment of silence. He started to cry. He told us that the doctor advised him to undergo an operation for his kidney. He refused though. He knew how costly it could be. He was aware that his family couldn't afford it with their small bakery as a source of income.

He continued crying. Ate Marivic shared words of encouragement and I just listened silently not knowing what to say. Mang Andoy said that he was not sure of what should he say. Kuya Rolly explained that through repentance and acceptance of the Lord Jesus.

Mang Andoy agreed for the second time to pray the prayer of acceptance. He was determined then to ask God's forgiveness for his sins. After that, we prayed the God would heal Mang Andoy. The way he held our hands revealed his sincerity. Mang Andoy got his second chance.

He agreed to see us the following week to continue the BS. Though his eyes were full of tears, he was filled with joy. He was holding my hands so tight as we bid our goodbyes. The said week came. We had our 2 other BS planned for the same day. After the two BS, we took a break. We found a small store, so we stayed there as we drink our soft drink and ate our cream-o.

As we approached the house of Mang Andoy, we saw a black curtain hanging near their place. A woman approached us and said that Mang Andoy died the other night. Mang Andoy lay down in the casket. I was surprised to him for the third time... and this time, not in the corner of the streets or even in their small sofa.

I was sad though I knew that I should feel otherwise --- Mang Andoy accepted the Lord Jesus before he died. Maybe I just look forward seeing him again, healed from his sickness and sharing with us his stories. I anticipated seeing him attending church and enjoying his new life serving God. And yes I hoped to ask him for an interview if he could share his testimony for this article. For weeks, I've thought of Mang Andoy's life. I was so affected, though I didn't know him so much. There were certain questions floating in my mind. I must admit that I didn't understand why sometimes God healed and sometimes not.

Weeks passed, I still continued in our BS. God was so faithful to make me realize that I missed a very important point. God gave Mang Andoy his second chance...and God was not unfair to call him in His presence. I was not able to see the other side of the story. God is giving every man chances to confess their sins and turned to Him.

I may never understand God's way but for sure it is for good. I can no longer interview Mang Andoy to share his testimony for the Lord. I may not write the other stories he had to tell. But one thing was sure; God had already written his story. And his death was not the end of the story but just the beginning of another chapter of eternal life with the Author and Finisher, our GOD.

I shared this precious experience with the youth group that Jeremy was handling. That was so many years ago, but whenever I remember Mang Andoy and how God saved him, no praises could ever equal God's love and forgiveness.

After the session, the youth left and I started to prepare my things. The day was so beautiful and it gave me so much hope for the future. I hold onto my necklace. I didn't notice that Jeremy was standing in front of me.

"Faith, thank you for the sharing how are you doing?"

"Oh, that was fast Jeremy."

"Yes, Kuya Ronnie volunteered to give the youth a ride. So, what's on that necklace? Have I miss something or what?"

"Oh, this is a couple's necklace!' I proudly said.

"A couple's necklace!"

"Yes!"

Jeremy looked at me intently.

"I'm so happy for you…and that smile on your face is priceless!"

"Thank you."

"So, tell me more about your story. I'm excited to hear everything."

"Well, that's a secret!" I kidded.

For the next hours, Jeremy asked me so many things about the journey that Gabriel and I had.

But as I looked back, it was all worth it. Waiting for him was not easy but I would still do it. Just one more year and we can be together.

"Do you miss him already Faith?" Jeremy asked me.

"I miss him," I answered.

"How much?"

"Immeasurable!" I said.

Epilogue

My True Love

My heart was beating so fast as I opened the door of the New Beginning Cafe. This is the day that I've been waiting for so long. Gabriel wanted to pick me up at home but I insisted that we should meet in the cafe already. I stood still and tried to compose myself. I was wearing a light green dress and my white doll shoes. I slowly opened the door, a soft music started to fill the air.

White and red petals of roses were beautifully scattered on the floor. I started to follow them. I knew that at the end of them, Gabriel would be waiting for me. He was holding a bouquet of white and red roses. Though I was still a few meters away from him, I saw that the tears from his eyes were about to fall. I felt the warm tears in my eyes as I continued to walk towards him. He was wearing a tuxedo. And he was really gorgeous and handsome.

I was only a meter away from Gabriel when he held out his hand to me. He let me sit on the beautiful wooden chair. He was on his knees as he pulled out a small silver box from his pocket.

"Faith Katherine Perez, will you be my beautiful wife and stay with me forever?" Gabriel asked me.

I couldn't answer back. I was so overwhelmed. But Gabriel patiently waited for my reply.

"Gabriel de Vega, I couldn't wait to have you as my dear husband. I'll stay with you forever!" I said.

Gabriel carefully put on the ring on my finger. I embraced him.

"I love you, my beautiful love," Gabriel whispered to my ears.

"I love you too my gorgeous love..."

I prayed that this moment would never end.

Suddenly the whole cafe was brightly lighted. And we heard fireworks outside. Gabriel took my hand as we ran outside. My parents, Rachel, Justin, Gabriel's mom. Ma'am Carmen and the children of the New Hope were all waiting for us.

I couldn't describe the joy within me. Gabriel put his arms around me as we watched the fireworks together with all the people we dearly love in our hearts. Finally, I am with my true love after so many years. Who would have thought that it would be Gabriel? He was my miracle.

"Number 3..." I whispered to Gabriel as I held his hand.

"Number 3?" Gabriel looked puzzled.

"Yes, remember... our bucket list?" I reminded him.

"Oh, Faith...I love you so much."

"I love you with all my heart Gabriel."

As if time stopped. Gabriel and I looked at each other. I could only see him. I could only hear his heartbeat as he moved closer and embraced me.

"Love suffers long and is kind; love does not envy; love does not parade itself, is not puffed up; does not behave rudely, does not seek its own, is not provoked, thinks no evil; does not rejoice in iniquity, but rejoices in the truth; bears all things, believes all things, hopes all things, endures all things.

Love never fails. But whether there are prophecies, they will fail; whether there are tongues, they will cease; whether there is knowledge, it will vanish away. For we know in part and we prophesy in part. But when that which is perfect has come, then that which is in part will be done away.

When I was a child, I spoke as a child, I understood as a child, I thought as a child; but when I became a man, I put away childish things. For now we see in a mirror, dimly, but then face to face. Now I know in part, but then I shall know just as I also am known.

And now abide faith, hope, love, these three; but the greatest of these is love." (1 Corinthians 13:4-13 NKJV)

I am Faith and this is my story...I'm so blessed and honored to share with you this journey of faith, hope and love, until the end. Praise be to God.

-end-

1 Corinthian 13:13 NIV
(Artwork by Hanna San Jose)

Acknowledgements

My utmost thanksgiving to our Lord and Savior Jesus Christ. All things were made possible because of Him.

Thanks to my Nanay and Tatay, Charing and Bob, my brothers and sisters. Special thanks to Gelo, Zybrey, Marcus and Andy.

My sincerest gratitude to my friends Melissa Licong, Prima Diaconte, May Advincula, Jayson Reyes, Loiue Mercado, Tess Devonshire, Lhen Paredes, Rose Cuneta, Rhodora Bercero, Daisy Patino, Hanna San Jose, and Dulce Badong.

To Samaritan's Place's kids and staff, to my dear mentors Dr. Marc and Marilen Morris, thank you so much for all your encouragement and inspiration.

Thank you Hanna San Jose for your wonderful artworks and Malaya Genotiva for the photo. Thank you WestBow Press team for all your help!

My sincerest gratitude to all my patient readers and fellow believers in Christ.

It's my joy to humbly share with you this work and the goodness of our Lord and Savior Jesus Christ. All the praises and honor belongs only to our Forever Love.

About the Author

Ihrilyn D. Pendatun lives in the Philippines. She uses the pen name Irena Faith. She accepted the Lord Jesus Christ as her personal Lord and Savior in year 2001. Since then, her life was changed. She continuously follows and seeks the heart of Jesus Christ in everything she does. She expresses her love for God through poetry and writing.

Follow her at https://www.wattpad.com/user/irenafaith or email her @fallen_leaves1214@yahoo.com